The Iguana Speaks My Name

~ ii ~

The Iguana Speaks My Name
a novella

Plus

Ten Backyard Stories From Panimache

By
Roberto Moulun

Published by EgretBooks.com
Laredo, Texas

$14.95 US

COPYRIGHT 2012, EGRETBOOKS.COM

THE IGUANA SPEAKS MY NAME © 1993, ROBERTO MOULUN, M.D.
TEN BACKYARD STORIES FROM PANIMACHE © 1996, ROBERTO MOULUN, M.D.

FRONT COVER ORIGINAL ART: © 2012, JORGINA JURY
BACK COVER ORIGINAL ART: © 1999, C. ENGEBRETSON

PRINTED IN USA

LIBRARY OF CONGRESS CONTROL NUMBER: 2012943686
    THE IGUANA SPEAKS MY NAME / ROBERTO MOULUN — 1ST ED.

ISBN 978-0-9857744-0-0

EGRETBOOKS.COM, 2163 LIMA LOOP, PMB 071-409, LAREDO, TX 78045, WWW.EGRETBOOKS.COM

EGRETBOOKS.COM IS A MEMBER OF THE INDEPENDENT BOOK PUBLISHERS ASSOCIATION, 1020 MANHATTAN BEACH BLVD, SUITE 204, MANHATTAN BEACH, CA, 90266, WWW.IBPA-ONLINE.ORG

Dedication

In memory of my friend Gardner McKay in Hawaii and the crew of my boat *Seafire*.

Seafire Under Sail

Table of contents

Introduction
Editor's Preface
Acknowledgments

Part One: The Iguana Speaks My Name

Part Two: Ten Backyard Stories From Panimache

Bibliography

Introduction: A Brief Interview With The Author

By Ed Tasca

Imagine a many-angled figment of face and form from Picasso.

As a dedicated, practicing psychiatrist for over sixty years, Roberto Moulun told me during an interview he granted me, that he agreed with the current mainstream conception of human psychology and creativity: *Within each human mind different selves are continually in conflict, fighting against one another for control. Expressions of art and humor are often the only thing capable of having them all talk peace.*

First impressions describe Roberto as a gentle, compassionate, diminutive man, who took on a career aimed at providing relief and compassion for human suffering in all its many mental and physical states. But looking closer, I discovered a man quite capable of fierce combat. At the same time Roberto made his decision to become a doctor and provide thoughtful, empathic counseling to those struggling with mental anguish and grief, he also decided to take on the entire prevailing medical establishment in Mexico City decades ago and shame them for what he considered criminal conduct.

"They did surgery on healthy dogs in order to practice removing and treating organs," Roberto explained to me, acting out his incredulity. "It was common practice. But I objected so strongly that I was able to have the practice stopped everywhere." Then, with no hint of conceit, he goes on shyly, "There is something so pure about a dog. You know they say when dogs die, they become angels for orphan children." There was an adversarial twinkle in his hazy brown eyes when he concluded, "I couldn't let them do that. I'm a devoted animal lover."

At the same time, peeking out from those very same eyes, another worldlier Roberto emerged during the interview, as he described his love of yacht racing with a bold, fiery spiritedness. (This is a sport requiring fierce competitiveness, focus and a skill at manipulating powerful natural forces.) It was this same fierce sense of purpose, one immediately understands, that drove Roberto to spend many years in the thick of world disasters, bringing physical and mental relief to traumatized earthquake and flood victims and workers–notably, pitting himself again in another struggle with powerful natural forces.

Further enriching and at the same time compounding Roberto's profile was a vexing spiritual side. Roberto confessed that he still believed in the Catholicism he learned as a child. "I aspire to a life comparable to the loving and forgiving Jesus," he explained to me. He then went on to surprise again by contending he didn't think he was capable of either of those Christian virtues.

But even more bewildering, he followed that intriguing comment with the complaint that I did not ask him the one question he had prepared for our interview. "You didn't ask me what my favorite food is."

And so I asked. He proceeded to extol the wonders of *bacalao al ojo arriero,* (a little-known cod dish native to Spain). It was then that I understood the importance of the question. Roberto was telling me what he believed to be his real heritage, his real identity. "I am a Spaniard," he said with a spike in tone that could have come from a conquistador. "I think I am a man of extreme passion," he declared, as though it were part of his Spanish brand. What's more, his mother hailed from Spanish gentry. But yet again, like everything about Roberto, this Spanish identity also came with angles and tangents and twists as he continued to explain that: he's of French (his father's side) *and* Spanish bloodlines, has an upbringing among the indigenous peoples of Guatemala, an advanced education in Mexico, a career spent largely in English-speaking America, and a scientific mind that is essentially international–all of which adds to the extraordinary human complexity present in the story-telling you will find here in Roberto's new book, *The Iguana Speaks My Name.*

However, after all the many influences one might expect on Roberto's writing, considering his multi-faceted provenance and personality, when one looks at this wonderful collection of stories, one will find that distinctly Spanish brand in the lyricism and naturalness of his language, a parallel to the simple yet poetic

Spanish of Don Cervantes. There are no affectations, no florid turns, just damn good writing about interesting characters and subtle, tantalizing storylines. The workmanship is a testament to Roberto's profound understanding of human nature and his artistry as a storyteller. It is no surprise that he has won three *El Ojo del Lago* awards for fiction, more than any other Lakeside writer; and that he did this in what he calls his "third" language, English.

Editor's Preface

This is a first edition book of works by master storyteller Roberto Moulun, born in Guatemala to French and Spanish parents. It is an extraordinary collection written in English, and is part of the Legacy Series at EgretBooks.com.

The Iguana Speaks My Name is a novella set in a time of guerilla warfare in Guatemala; *Ten Backyard Stories From Panimache* is a collection of charming and witty village tales timeless in nature. Like the author, the stories are full of insight and understanding and love for the culture and people in villages of Central America. Ultimately the stories are lessons about life learned through experiences close up and face-to-face -- haunting tales of hope and despair, happiness and sadness -- full of magical realism reminiscent of Isabel Allende, and enhanced with the author's fondness for great literature and art and music and wine.

I first met Roberto in 2011 during a winter vacation at Lake Chapala, a Mexican mecca for expatriates from the USA and Canada, many of whom have turned to writing and art in retirement.

"This guy is a great storyteller and a helluva good writer," said Richard, my former neighbor from Maryland who had retired to the area. Both of them met me at breakfast in Ajijic the next week, before the twice-monthly meeting of Lake Chapala writers.

Roberto was showing his age—decades etched in the crevasses on his brown face framed by unruly gray hair.

"*Café correcto*," he told the waiter, a contagious smile tugging at the corners of his mouth. A mug of black coffee appeared in a couple of minutes, "corrected" by the waiter who knew just how much tequila Roberto preferred.

Richard guided us through almost an hour of my learning about Roberto's impressive background, including hanging out with adventurer/actor Gardner McKay in Hawaii and winning a blue-water sailing championship. We met again two weeks later and Roberto handed me a manila folder of his stories printed by *El Ojo del Lago*, a monthly publication at Lake Chapala. After sizing up each other in a few more meetings we shook hands across the table on a tentative deal, and he gave me a well-worn black leather satchel with these two unpublished manuscripts from the 1990's.

"Those are the only print copies he has, and the computer files are corrupted," Richard told me. "Don't lose them."

One thing I learned early in editing Roberto's works: do not change ANYTHING without his reluctant approval. For that reason, the dialogue and quotations from literature are exactly the way the characters speak and remember, although slightly different from what online research shows.

After lunch at an outdoor restaurant on the village plaza one day that winter, Roberto gave me a glimpse of his philosophy of life in retirement: "Ajijic is God's waiting room," he said, gesturing toward octogenarians sitting in the tropical sun on nearby park benches, five-thousand-feet high in the Sierra Madre mountains.

Hopefully, there will be more stories from Roberto while he is waiting, and maybe I will be fortunate enough to help publish more of his work. However, none will be as special to me as the stories in this book.

The Legacy Series at EgretBooks.com comprises literary works conveying a broader awareness of cultural heritage.

Partial funding for the Legacy Series comes from the estate of Helen May Miller, a native of the Missouri Ozarks, who began her career in the early 1940's working at libraries in Arkansas, Maryland, Missouri, and on military bases in Germany and England. After returning to the United States in 1957 she pursued her career at state libraries in West Virginia and Idaho, serving almost nineteen years as the Idaho State Librarian before retiring in 1980. Over the years she sampled diverse cultures while travelling extensively across the USA, in Canada and Mexico, and in Europe and Asia.

A memoriam about her dedication to making great books available to the public is on the Internet at http://www.idaholibraries.org/idlibrarian/index.php/idaho-librarian/article/viewFile/67/202

EgretBooks.com provides a home for independent authors whom traditional publishers overlook, and uses digital technology to provide worldwide access to books that might not otherwise be published.

~ Mikel Miller, Managing Editor, EgretBooks.com

~ xvi ~

Acknowledgements

I want to thank Mikel Miller for bringing this book to fruition, fellow writer Ed Tasca for writing the introduction, and Jorgina Jury for producing the original artwork for the front cover.

I also want to thank two steadfast friends in Ajijic -- Richard Stafford, the catalyst for the book project; and Dudley Baker, longtime friend and an investment advisor.

Lastly I want to thank Alejandro Grattan-Dominguez, editor of *El Ojo del Lago*, who has printed several of my stories.

Thanks again to all of you, and to the many others who encouraged me along the way.

-- Roberto Moulun, M.D.

Come away, O human child:
To the waters and the wild
With a fairy, hand in hand,
For the world's more full of weeping
Than you can understand.

-William Butler Yeats

PART ONE:

THE IGUANA
SPEAKS MY NAME

I

LA CHINA

My house was well-weathered, hardened and scarred by sun, wind and hail. But it had a grace and beauty that withstood, no matter how badly the weather treated it, no matter how neglected it had been through the years. You couldn't tell that from the inside, though. The inside was comfortable and warm, with paneling of oak and hard tropical woods. The floor was a firm reddish brown of Spanish tiles, and the fireplace was surrounded by stonework from San Lucas, where the best of stone cutters still take pride in their craft.

The living room opened onto the garden, which was larger than it needed to be. It made my house look like someone wearing a dress too large, even if it was a pretty dress, printed with daisies, fuchsia, red bougainvillea, and very green leaves resembling the paws of a giant tiger. They called them *trepadoras*, because they climbed and drank their strength from the trees, which didn't seem to mind the embrace. The soil was rich and kind and could feed both. There were not many butterflies. It was not the season for them. It was getting cold, with Christmas already hiding around the corner.

A red gate led onto the street. To open it was like cracking a pomegranate of children and yellow dogs, clinging to each other with spit and runny noses and barking and happy squealing and mean snarling.

You then stepped onto the hard cobblestones of Calle Cuatro de Febrero, which was the official name of our street. It was not a good name for the street. It had been given in mournful memory of the victims of the earthquake, which devastated the town on that date. But no one ever called it that. The street was known as Calle del Farolito, because of the house of the little red light–the only cathouse in the village–located on the corner of the street, proclaiming that life, no matter how sinful, beats death by a long margin.

The villagers didn't like sadness and went to extremes to exorcize it. Firecrackers sold better than maize. The evangelical missionaries, with their guitars, had a heyday, and even took over Saturday nights. The loud music–louder still through the speakers of the mission truck by the lake–yelled to everyone that Jesus loves you. Hallelujah! The traditional church with its Catholic novenas stood empty, except for a group of sober Alcoholics Anonymous attendees who looked miserable as they gathered there, like bats in daylight.

The street merchants in their matchbox stalls hung the typical fabrics as if they were the flags of myriad new nations. It was a bright display of tropical colors–which soon became pale and worn out in the ever-constant dust–while the merchants rested from the fatigue of hoping that a customer would stop to buy.

Somewhere a war was being fought. Distant gunfire coughed every so often. Fear spread among the villagers like the smell of fruit fermented in the sun, waiting to be swept away with giggles and lies: "It is only firecrackers in Santa Lucia.... They are celebrating the fiesta of their saint."

The land bled from a war no one wanted to notice. The people went about their business smiling in bliss, like the Fool of the Tarot about to step into the abyss. Once a day, in the morning, a heavy military truck drove across town toward the lake bringing replacement troops for the outposts. The young soldiers rode in the open back, looking as happy as the children in front of my house, holding their guns with the joy of a child who has gotten its first toy. As I saw them go by, I wondered what their enemies could have looked like.

El Farolito wasn't much of a cathouse. The outside was fenced with wooden boards like a baseball field. The thick, wooden gate was seldom open. One never saw anything going on. Even the music that played at night was subdued, as if it were embarrassed to be heard. The yard was as barren as the playground of the Benedictine monastery in Solola, except for a few chickens that pecked here and there. Every so often one would pretend to have found a worm and run away from the others until cornered. Then the disillusioned fowl would return to their scratching and sifting of the dust.

The little wooden house was painted white and blue, like a rural school. It had a row of gaudy lights nailed to the roof, which made it look like a village girl prettied up with ribbons in her hair.

Of all the women in the house, and there were four of them, La China had the worst reputation. She was different. Rather pretty with the slender figure of her Chinese ancestors. When they all sang together or when they danced, she stood out like a damselfly in a cluster of bees. When I first met her, I thought she looked like Olympia in the painting by Manet, but it wasn't easy to imagine the artist's elegant courtesan in such poor surroundings as this.

It didn't help that she had a child. Little Rolando was not good for the whoring business; customers grow shy in front of children.

Except for the patronage of soldiers, El Farolito would have been in dire economic straits.

Morning is not a good time for cats or whores. La China was standing by the door under the sign that advertised Cerveza el Cabro, with a painting of a charging ram. She watched her child pick up sticks and rocks and struggle in his attempts to walk. Her dress was the color of an old rat and in the shape of a bell, but that didn't hide her sensuality. Her thick black hair covered half her face like a veil, which she lifted to smile at me. She liked to chat. Our short conversations flew away like bits of paper in the morning breeze.

"Hola, vas al café?" she asked.

"First to the post office."

"With Alizarin?"

"Good guess."

"He doesn't get his letter still?"

"Not yet; perhaps today."

"I doubt it. So, when are you going to come and convert me?"

"I will not even try. You know what happens to men who try to convert women."

"Like the Reverend Davidson, you mean, the one who cut his throat over that working girl with the loud music? Was it Sadie? I remember."

She did. Remember. I had told her the story by Maugham: "Rain."

"You got it right."

"I believe he was afraid of facing his wife."

"Why would you say so, China?"

"Men never kill themselves because of their own conscience but because others force their conscience on them."

"You may have something there, China."

"Someday you and I must talk seriously about the things I know."

"*Otro dia*; not today."

"*Esta bien, otro dia,* some other day, but I really want to..."

"*Entiendo. Bonito dia, no?*"

"*Muy bonito. Ve con Dios.*"

"*Gracias. Ciao.*"

She smiled prettily and busied herself with Rolando. I went on to Calle Santander.

The street was plagued by vicissitudes. Alizarin called them so, from the French *vicissitude* that implied not only a change but also calamity. He was an artist from San Jean de Luz who spoke with a strong accent from *le pays basque* and translated his phrases from French. (Speaking with him, you felt like you had mastered a foreign language.) The source of calamity was a nest of bicycles gathered like praying mantises. Every so often, a villager would get on his bike and ride away, pumping the pedals with ferocious determination. He rode, staring straight ahead in paralyzed delight of speed, expecting the bicycle to know its way home as their donkeys had in the recent past. One seldom sees horses or donkeys anymore, but the hybrid bicycles swish by, scattering people about them. Oh, for the return of *el burro!*

Alizarin and I were pedestrians every day; it was his *via crucis* to the post office, which opened at mid-day, hoping to get a letter from his woman in Germany. Everyone knew about the letter that never seemed to arrive. There were bets and guesses between Don Cosme, the postmaster–who had a tinted black mustache and smelled of anisette–and his young assistant.

I always waited for Alizarin in the atrium of the old Franciscan church, which stood frowning but amused, a colonial gem of Churriguera, across from the *Oficina de Correos.*

"Y bien?"

"No letter."

"Quieres tomar un café?"

"C'est bien."

Al Chisme was our usual cafe. It had a small patio that opened to the street, yawning in the slow afternoon. We could watch the village life parading by, followed by aimless dogs.

"Do you think she has ceased to love me?"

His love and pain were incongruous, almost a pretense. His hair had grayed at an early age. Maybe he had missed ever being young. Now he wished to color his life with romance as Don Cosme did with his mustache.

"Maybe she is ill and cannot write."

"She could ask someone to write for her."

"Maybe a new love."

"Impossible! She could be carrying my child!" He hoped no one else could love her if she were with child. So deep was his despair. So damnable and useless!

"Send a cablegram," I said. "Ask: 'Why the silence?' It is only three words."

"That is excellent. I could do it in French– *'Pourquoi le silence?'* Isn't it more poetic?"

"C'est pas donne'," I said. "Does she speak French?"

"No."

"Then?"

"She could ask a nurse to read it to her."

"Is she in a hospital?"

He raised both hands toward his shoulders in a helpless gesture. "*Alors là!* How would I know? I feel like Theseus lost in the labyrinth."

He remained lost in his labyrinth for quite some time while I played crossword puzzles with my thoughts, sorting bits of my life, which didn't fit into words that would make any sense. Soon my memories ran off, as watercolors do if one is not careful, and I had only feelings left without the forms that would make it possible to show them to others. I felt sad with his sadness, because it is in the nature of love and friendship that one can live the other's fate. I wished he could shake his anguish as a dog shakes the water off after falling into the sea.

"I saw La China today," I said. "She asked about you."

"A good woman," Alizarin said.

"But many people think of her as a bad woman," I said, almost asking.

"I trust her. That is what I meant."

"You trust her." I repeated what he had said as if it were incomplete. "Would you let her keep your money?"

"*Jamais!* Never. She would squander it and think nothing of it. But she could keep my best painting for me."

"Wouldn't she sell it and spend the money?"

"No."

Not much I could say to that. Alizarin wasn't selling any paintings these days anyway. He had to bake bread to make ends meet. At least, the bread sold well.

"Would she keep a secret?" I asked.

"Only to the limit of her heart. One should never trust her with too terrible a secret."

He was slowly coming out of his gloom, as if following a thread from the maze of his aloneness.

Then, with untimely impertinence, a shot exploded! A child soldier held his rifle away from himself, startled by his own blunder.

"*El tiro se me fue*; the bullet escaped!" he repeated over and over in a litany of helplessness.

The day collapsed with heaviness as if it had lost its will to live in the dusty village.

I felt the emptiness of a man who had no secret to share, no thirst nor hunger nor fear. Not even pain.

I saw the villagers gather around, smiling as they always did.

I heard one say: "There were two old men drinking coffee. And then one of them died."

II

SKETCHES

We didn't die. The stray bullet had wasted itself against the wall breaking a scab of plaster. Alizarin had fallen backwards, startled by the shot. He grinned from the floor as if being shot were part of his daily life. *"Barron-nous,"* he blurted, smacking the back of one hand with the flat of the other. "Let's get out of here!" He started to get up, but sat down again.

"Alors, les flics," he said pointing to the door.

A corporal had arrived. Seriously, he proceeded to dig the bullet from the wall with his knife. He snatched the rifle from the young soldier to compare the caliber. He then thrust the weapon back at him.

"Deberian ahorcarte por estupido!" he snapped at him. He then turned, smiling warmly to Alizarin and helped him up.

"Have you compliments?" he asked politely.

I guessed he meant complaints.

"No," I replied. "No compliments."

The corporal smiled warmly. He turned to Alizarin and handed him the fragment of lead.

"Having for lock," he said. Then he spoke to the soldier. "Sorri dee American," he ordered.

The child soldier didn't understand. He looked bewildered, resting his chin on the muzzle of his gun that was almost as tall as he was.

The people who had gathered moved away as if awakening from a dream. They talked in somnambulistic bits and pieces.

"He only fell backwards."

"Move on *muchacho*. They don't know what to say anymore; it is the government."

"...Don't say government aloud, don't say *tonterias*; talking nonsense can land you in jail."

"To jail as an *agitador* and *borracho*..."

"*Borracho?* He must have been drunk, the old man; I should have guessed."

"They are intemperate and agitators and blame the government and the people."

"They should stay in their own *pais* if they are going to be intemperate!"

The sounds got softer and faded into the distant barking of dogs. There followed the sound of wind. It was the afternoon wind that the *Cakchickel* call *Xocomil*. The wind that carries away sin. And, as if to confirm a baptism with water, rain clouds came over, and a downpour washed the town clean.

Once more people were happy with the joy of children on their way home from school; young women who sold flowers in the market behind the church now were returning home with live chickens and green watercress and little red radishes.

There was a *Cakchickel* woman, dressed in the blue and red colors of her village, with a design on her blue skirt of their totem coral snake. She sat by a large basket of *anacates,* wicked looking mushrooms the color of ripe tangerines.

"It is dangerous to eat wild mushrooms. Sometimes whole families get wiped out because of the poison," Alizarin said.

"Not mine, *Tata*. I pick them myself."

Then she looked in the opposite direction to indicate she was offended.

I bought two bags–four handfuls that was–weighed in a balance made of two small baskets, a string, and a copper weight. We added *anacates* until the baskets were even, and we kept adding more of the evil parasites as if we were weighing the sins of humanity. She was pleased but too proud to show that she was. She feigned indifference. But then, with the grace of a coquette giving alms, she added one more handful of the mushrooms.

"*Tu ganancia, Tata...your gain.*"

Then again she looked away, back to the past, when she was the queen of a thousand Maya warriors, dressed in resplendent emerald green feathers of *quetzal*.

She had a head start on me. She knew the land, and magic helped her tread lighter. I also made it to *Chimultic,* the pyramid amid the green mountains where maidens had jumped into the abyss to the *Zenote,* an eye of blue water where the gods bathed. She had not been chosen for the young gods but to keep the race going into time, and to plant maize and bear children.

She had called me *Tata* because I was older than she, and a man. Yet I knew that she would die long before me, when she was fifty-seven or maybe fifty-three or perhaps forty-seven, because the Maya die of many reasons. A hot illness or a cold illness, an illness from fright or from sadness, or the soul can leave or be stolen or lured away.

"Then one dies," the *sajorin* Sun Tat had said, "because one cannot live without the warmth from within." He had lived many years but then he was a *sajorin*, a witch. He had been called from his village, farther than Santa Catarina, to tell about a child, a new-born girl who failed to thrive. The mother was perplexed and believed her milk was weak. She tormented herself with guilt and shame in front of the father who gave her the best food and vitamins that he had bought from the pharmacist.

They wouldn't believe me when I told them even the child of the North American President Kennedy could be like their daughter; guilt stood by them like a sentinel, and that is why we called the *sajorin* Sun Tat from his village farther away than Santa Catarina, in Palopo.

El sajorin had read the luck in the smoke of *pum* and scattered red beans, which he had gotten somewhere from a vine in the jungle where the heat is cruel and one meets vipers and tigers, and the water reaches in brooks and streams painted in fall colors by leaves that fall from the trees long before their time, like the virgins of the Maya, and where waterfalls stretch their nakedness with the unashamed abandon of women who no longer care what they may be called because they know their fate is to bring life in the tropics where procreation is always a sin. There is no respect for punctuation in the jungle. Not good or bad, but heat and jungle and life rutting, as if man were just beginning to learn the wisdom of knowledge from the tree where the snake seduced Eve, and there are gods who still care what animals do when they are alone in the night.

"Her soul doesn't wish to abide," the sajorin had said and pointed to a hummingbird, a *Huitzizilin,* who wouldn't alight for long.

It wasn't quite the same, but we had understood that a soul could leave on its own will.

"Ask them if they wish for me to convince her to stay."

I asked the parents, the grandmother and the oldest of the aunts. They wished it so, and the ceremony was made ready for the following day. Torches of pine were lit in the four corners of the yard, one for each of the points of the horizon. Then we waited for the sun to rise. With the first light he took the child in his arms and sprinkled water on her head, saying in Spanish: "Oh, my child, take and receive the water which is our life and is given for the renewing of our body. It is to wash and purify, and may these drops enter your body and stay there, that they may destroy the evil and sin which was given to you before the beginning of the world, because we are the children of *Chalchivitlycue,* who is queen of the waters."

Sun Tat then washed the child and said: "Whosoever comes that be hurtful to this child, leave her and depart from her, for she lives anew and is born anew now, as she is purified and cleaned afresh, and our mother *Chalchivitlycue* again brings the child into the world."

He then raised the child to the sun.

"Grant this child your inspiration, since you are the great god, and the great goddess is with you."

He then turned to the child and admonished: "You now will answer to the name Huitzitziling. That is your name, your companion and your messenger to the goddess, because she sent it to us when we were in the dark about your life."

The child was given to the parents, crying with anger and hunger, biting her mother's breast as she fed. The father stared in wonder.

Sun Tat called me aside. "Tell them to move away into the mountains. The forces from the lake are jealous and will lure her soul again. They thirst for children."

Maybe that is what happened.

"You are distracted *comme un fou de l'asile de Sainte Anne*," said the mocking French voice.

I left my reverie and the *Cachickel* woman. I followed her in my thoughts as one walks a friend down the road for a farewell. Then I went with Alizarin into an alley ridged with hibiscus and guava trees and papaya and mango, and over a bridge of wood bitten by weather to his house, a comic construction of adobe, whitewashed like the face of a mime.

III

ASTARTE

There were four canvases displayed on the white walls, of such bright beauty that it appeared more like four butterflies held there by pins of silver or by pins of gold. They were his paintings of the three volcanoes by the lake—San Pedro, Toliman and Atitlan. Alizarin had drawn them not with the fine lines of nature but with the abrupt and sharp angles the *Tzutuhil,* encountered when they worked their soil or walked in their valleys and canyons.

They still lived there, the *Tzutuhil*, even though their gods were in hiding. But gods outlast time.

"What does that mean?" Alizarin asked.

I had been thinking aloud, without knowing it, and now faced the task of explaining.

"Gods have no beginning and no end; time is nothing to them. Men's tears or laughter mean nothing to them; they are capricious, like a coquette who hides behind a mask. One never knows when she will take it off and reveal her beauty, or even if she will, but one hopes until midnight. Now, one says, she must; it is after all the time of disclosure when the grain will be separated from the chaff! But the coquette has left the party with the worst sinner from out of town."

"I don't always understand your metaphors," Alizarin said. "Is it then that you don't believe in virtue?"

"Not as a source of reward."

He shrugged his shoulders in Gallic indifference and brought from his bedroom two more canvases, which he set by the window. They were not as good as the others; he had painted them in poor light. His window faced south, and his colors conveyed violence. His volcanoes would have been vulgar but for the gentleness of his brushwork. A light touch, as if a woman had held his hand.

There were other canvases lined against the wall, but they had their gray backs turned to the sun, hiding their faces as uniformed school girls did when the nuns brought them to the park on Sundays, and they saw me approach. I remembered their aroma of mint and marjoram.

In a corner of the room where two walls met at the west, a black widow spider worked at her net, a red kerchief tied to her waist, with the intensity of a Jamaican sorceress casting a spell.

"She is Astarte," Alizarin said, "my spider. I shall paint her as Kali with her six giving hands."

"Why Astarte?" I asked.

"It goes far back in time," he explained. "She was the last of the goddesses. After Theseus killed the Minotaur and, with her kingdom lost, she went into hiding. Men thought she had left for good, but she returned as Astarte, the Phoenician. Her rites no longer demanded the sacrifice of men, but the heroes no longer believed in her. They prayed and sacrificed only to male gods."

He was busy bringing from the cabinet a bottle of *Pouilly Fuissé* and a tin of *pâté de foie gras truffé*, gifts from a woman admirer in America, he explained, delighted with his own magnificence. He brought out bread he had baked that morning from his mother's recipe back in Labastide.

It was good to be there in his studio and to hear him talk of ancient religions and old rites. The smell of turpentine and fresh oil paints will always be the most compatible if one is sipping a burgundy and biting into French bread and *pâté de foie*, when one sits on a chair of noble wood, resting one's arms on a round table, where space has been made by moving aside books that tell of the Upanishads.

"You know," he said with renewed interest, "there is presently a revival of the wicca, the old religion of women who revered the earth as a mother and the horned god, the magic stag, as the consort."

"The devil?" I asked.

"They called him so, in the middle ages, and the name became a symbol for every evil, but the wicca insists he was maligned. He was the consort to the goddess, and his was the realm of the four points–the air, water, fire, and earth. Each had a throne on the horizon. The earth occupied the north; her symbol was the bull, and her power was manifested in winter, when the consort was born from death. It bespoke of death and rest. The air was spring; eagle and birds were her symbols. The consort falls in love with her, but the goddess of the east eludes him. They meet again in the noon of summer, in the south. They mate and their symbol is the lion.

"Then comes fall, not an easy season for men or trees," Alizarin continued. "There is harvest, of course, but a sense of decline. At sundown the consort dies. Serpents and dolphins play in the water. It is the last moon until the moon of winter when the witches throw their web to form the magic pentacle of power."

Alizarin had delivered his long discourse with an unusual display of emotion.

"You seem quite taken," I said, wishing to break the spell that seemed so seductive in the sunset. "I know it is not always easy to dislike the devil, after all: 'of all the spirits that deny, the mocking jester bothers me the least.'"

"Is it, then, that you have read Goethe?" posed Alizarin with pleasure.

He had recognized the quote, however imperfect.

"Faust is a vindication of the devil. In fact, Goethe depicts him as a gentleman of honor who keeps his word even in adversity, a German of the best sort, Heidelberg through and through."

"If this is your wish," I said, "I solemnly affirm the devil to be a German."

We stood up dramatically, brought our glasses together and for a moment believed every word of our toast in the magic of Burgundy.

We could have been in Paris at one of the cafes on the left bank or, Alizarin said, at Saint Jean de Luz, watching the fishing boats return with the low tide, or better still, at Labastide D'Armanaque, his beloved village in Gascogne.

"I have a son there," he said. "His name is Hercules."

Maybe it was the wine, but I also wished to talk about myself and my loves, and of towns and streets, with smells and colors, fresh and rich as a Pizarro, but I was detained by shyness, the clumsy shyness of a hermit crab changing shells, half shyness and half fear lest a predator may know the secret and attack.

"There is a village in Malaga which I love," I said at last. "Benalmadena, a Moorish town with white houses and blue skies. Time walks very slowly there among the olive trees and the cobblestones. The air, as one breathes, brings life and a desire to live.

"There is a fountain in the center of town. It is the only one in the world, I believe, that has a statue of a young woman peeing. She holds a shell, and from it the water overflows into the fountain."

"In truth?" Alizarin interrupted in amusement. *"Une statue d'une jeune fille qui fait pipi?"*

"In truth," I insisted wishing I had said it in French. "It is a lovely fountain. The statue is innocent like a young Astarte. She was a child from the village, filling the fountain with her water, unconcerned with others, attentive only to the shell, showing it proudly and with care, lest it should spill.

"Who was the artist, the sculptor?"

"I didn't ask; it didn't even occur to me to ask. I was traveling with friends. I wished for them to see a bullfight and there was one–a Goyesca–in Benalmadena. It turned out very different from what I had planned. The bulls refused to fight and sat in their corners perhaps declaiming Walter Starkie's soliloquy for the bulls in Villafranca: "Dear folks: this is a fiesta and the sun is shining. You are all gaily disporting yourselves; why kill me? Let me off this boring exhibition of myself and send me away to a quiet meadow where I can chew the cud."

It was just as well because Antonio, the first matador, was late in getting to the arena. He had fought in Venezuela the previous day and suffered jet lag. He himself wished to chew the cud. The band played vigorously, and listening to the festive music was as close as we got to watching a fight.

That evening we had dinner where toreros and newspaper people gathered. My friends showed no respect; the Rioja wine was to blame. They happily kept comparing the noble heads of Miura and Urquijo, the aristocrats of fighting bulls that lined the walls as trophies, with Van Gogh because they had lost their ears. I was almost in despair when Alfonso, the torero, took me aside."

"Una mala tarde, la tenemos todos," he said, regretting the poor fight. He then ordered two *manzanillas*, and drank to my health.

We heard him coming with the scattered bell-ringing of scared hens and whimpering half barks of timid dogs and all the signs that nature gives on the arrival of evil.

He was slender and tight like a whip, with hate and anger and cornered resentment as men know in defeat. He was a Salvadoran who had to leave his homeland and seek refuge in a foreign land to save his life. He was intoxicated with stories of battles and cruelty, guerrillas and injustice, and convinced that, except for himself and others like him, corruption and wickedness would destroy the land.

He recoiled from me.

"The paper American," he said, and I felt his hate slithering over me.

"Pascualillo glorified," I said, and got up to leave.

"Qui est el Pascualillo?" asked Alizarin in surprise.

"You must read *La Familia de Pascual Duarte*," I advised, with strange detachment, "a book by Cela. Pascualillo is a criminal who seeks for reasons to kill."

I heard the crash of the stranger's boot against the wall and the violent stomping.

"A poisonous spider!" he yelled.

I walked out to the yard and then into the road. Tropical flowers look different at night.

"So much for Astarte," I heard myself say.

IV

MARGARITA

Margarita was at the bridge, resting her arms on the parapet, looking at something that floated away in the river, half covered by mist, drizzle and darkness.

I realized she was away. She suffered from epilepsy, not convulsions but periods when she would be absent from all that surrounded her. In a world so intimate, only she was allowed in.

When she was there, all of us who knew the secret kept silent lest she be frightened into returning too soon, before she could forget and lose her soul, as they say happens to sleep walkers if awakened in the middle of their night journeys.

The shadow drifting in the river, each moment farther away as it followed the current, looked like a giant bat with wings outstretched, caught in a fluid web.

"No, too large for a bat," I whispered, to keep from waking her. "A vampire perhaps, not even a vampire. It is a raven or a black hawk, but no, the shadow is larger, a condor, that must be it, a condor who got lost on his flight to Los Andes and failed in his strength, now floats away toward drowning..."

I stood by Margarita in mournful vigil for a giant in defeat.

"It is Alizarin's umbrella," she said softly, as if talking to herself. "It flew out of my hands."

Then she started to laugh, at first lightly as a brook, and then like overflowing water.

She had returned none the worse, lovely in her ripe womanhood, and strong with the defiance of those accustomed to challenging ghosts.

"I was on my way to return his umbrella," she explained, "but it flew out of my hands and there was nothing I could do about it. Now it is gone, unless we go to Santa Catarina, where the river loops, and try to fish it out before it goes into the lake." Santa Catarina was five miles away.

Margarita pranced ahead of me, for her prancing was a manner of walking. She had learned the stride some fifteen years before as a majorette at Baton Rouge, Louisiana, where she went to learn English, and it had become second nature with her. Her boots were dated from those years; she had several pairs she resoled often. She couldn't drive and most of her errands had to be on foot.

A canter is to a gallop as a walk is to a trot, but less natural a step.

I recognized the voice of the Professor, the impertinent one, who haunted my most intimate moments with probing questions.

Is it then that you love her? he asked.

"I don't believe so; I hardly know her."

Then is it desire?

"Perhaps desire. But no, desire would only be a part of it; I'd rather be desired by her."

And you wish the desire fulfilled?

"Not yet, not for a long time, never if fulfillment would take her away, like looking back to see if Euridice is following!"

What is it then? the Professor asked, frustrated in his dialectic.

"It is," I answered, "whatever she wishes it to be."

"We will never catch up with the umbrella if you keep falling behind." It was a reproach but her voice was laughing as if she didn't care.

"We may have lost it already," I said. "Do crocodiles eat umbrellas?"

"They are known gluttons."

"There was a crocodile in Sarawac, which is in Borneo," I explained, "that swallowed a young woman. She was wearing her Christmas gifts, and that is how her husband, who was a hunter, knew he had avenged her and killed the right crocodile because he found a golden comb, something of a family heirloom, in its gullet."

"That is tragic and very gory," she protested insincerely.

"You don't have to believe it, but the story was told by the last Ranee of Sarawac, Lady Brooke, who was there at the time when it happened."

"Then I guess that I must believe it," she said in boredom, "but there aren't any crocodiles in this river; it's too high upland for them."

I felt chastised as if I had been petulant or somehow otherwise missed the boat, or perhaps she was now recovered from her moment of confusion and reproached me for having been a witness to it.

"Do you mind that I was there?" I asked guessing.

She slowed her step until I reached her.

"I always do," she said, "but with you I mind less."

We then walked side-by-side, letting our hands touch until we reached the bank where the river made a loop. We sat by a rock, and Margarita took off her boots to get ready for her walk into the river.

"This water is so cold," she said, "it could freeze a tentacle."

She had lovely feet, even if she called them tentacles. The darkness came flowing with the river. A handful of light bugs misfired like wet matches, and soon the cicadas, encouraged by our silence, raised their raspy voices.

So, I thought, this is how fools feel–and lovers.

We never meant to overhear them thrashing in their passion with the violence of despair.

He had taken off his belt with revolver, and the other, Felipe, the young soldier, had set his rifle against a tree, careful and dainty as a courtesan.

I thought I saw the shadow of a condor glide down the river. She brought her hand to my lips and held it there. I felt the agony of cold sweat in my face and chest and loins, and the salty taste of a primeval scream of horror that I didn't understand. I closed my eyes and waited, and waited with my lips to her hand until they left satiated, the sinners, in fear of Jehovah, Lord of warriors.

She then held my head to her breast, and I cried dark tears, without knowing why.

"Tomorrow," she murmured, "we still have tomorrow."

"Thank you," I said, to say something. "Thank you for bridling my fears."

"I didn't want you to scream and scare the children," she said.

We had just started back down the road when we were stopped by a patrol, a small group of soldiers dressed as caterpillars.

There is no longer glory or dignity in soldiering, I thought; gone are the bright uniforms, the reds of the Hussars, the blue of the Legion, the drums beating like hearts, the regimental colors and flags, the bugles and voices of command, the beliefs that went with it all. All we now have is this pathetic sample of adolescents dressed in fatigues the color of rot, as one finds in rain soaked forests, where centipedes and ugly vermin live.

I kept walking, ignoring them, and their platoon leader raised his rifle.

"*Alto*," he yelled. "Stop immediately!"

He had difficulties enunciating as if he were scared. It is not easy to speak when you carry a gun. There is fright in that kind of power. Men are not designed to be gods, not even minor ones, not even insignificant ones who can kill but not give life or consolation.

Then Margarita spoke.

"He is deaf. Don't you see?"

"*Sordo?*" the soldier asked and lowered his weapon.

"Very, very *sordo*," she said, "*sordo como una tapia.*"

Now there's a fancy expression, I thought: *Tapia*, a stone wall as one sees in the fields of Spain or Ireland– deaf as one of those walls. Very well then, so I kept walking, while the soldier ran in front of me waving his arms as peasants do when trying to prevent a stampede of milking cows. I couldn't help laughing.

He made signs for us to follow, as if he himself had become mute. I handed him my bag of *anacates* to carry and followed him for a short distance to their encampment, a small house of adobe and red brick with a pretty fire in the front yard. And that is how we met El Capitan Lobo, the military chief of the area. I had seen him before; at least I had seen his revolver, a .44 Colt. He noticed my glance.

"Not regulation," he said, "but I wear it as a privilege of rank." He smiled an engaging smile. "It was my grandfather's," he explained, "but it's still functional. Brings good luck."

"What are you doing here, Margarita?" he asked. "Not spying, I hope." He turned to me, as a husband explaining to his guest the foibles of a wife: "Many people suspect her of being with the guerrillas."

"Is she?" I asked.

"How would I know? I trained in counterinsurgency at Leavenworth, Kansas. Long word counterinsurgency, isn't it? They sent some of us to train there, but it was a sad waste. We don't have enemies here, only victims. Sometimes we massacre the Indians, other times it's the guerrillas. The victims are always the same–the Indians and the poor."

"Was it in Santa Catarina?" asked Margarita. "I heard a whole family got wiped out."

"A whole family," he confirmed. "Someone coveted their land. The guerrillas did it. Thank God! I would despise myself if we had done it."

He was tormented. We sat for a while with him by the fire in silence. I remembered La China warning me that behind his back people called him Capitan Coyote, not wolf, *lobo*, but *coyote;* you can never trust a *lobo*, she said, but "worse still" a *coyote*.

"We really must get going," Margarita said, as if we had just stopped by for tea. El Capitan turned to his assistant, who was still holding my bag of wild mushrooms. "They don't need papers; I know them. Are you carrying any weapons?" he asked me.

"We have some *anacates*," I said retrieving my bag. "You are welcome to them."

"Just what I always hoped for," said Lobo. "This could wipe out a whole regiment." Whatever else, Lobo had great charm.

"You must cook them with a little silver spoon or a silver coin," said Margarita. "If they don't turn black, the *anacates* are safe."

"I can have them tasted by my soldiers," said Lobo smiling.

"Either way," I said. "Enjoy."

"Thank you, pal," he said, as we turned to go. That, at least, seemed straight from Kansas.

V

CISCA

The morning woke up, crisp and pretty. I looked out my bedroom window to the paleness of the three volcanoes and the deep blue of the lake.

> *I wandered lonely as a cloud*
> *That floats on high o'er vales and hills,*
> *When all at once I saw a crowd,*
> *A host of golden daffodils*
> *Beside the lake, beneath the trees*
> *Fluttering and dancing in the breeze.*
>
> *Ten thousand saw I at a glance*
> *Tossing their heads in sprightly dance.*

I wished William Wordsworth could have been with me. What would he have written, I wondered, when the firecrackers announced m-a-r-k-e-t d-a-y, as if spelling with minimal explosions the happiest day of the week for the village.

As if a piñata had been broken in Calle Cuatro de Febrero, I watched the young and the old *Cakchikel*, their children, with their dogs, running in their clipped trot with baskets balancing on their heads, with tomatoes and white eggs, and spring onions, and with the rich smell of soap of Castile, and the freshness of

Indian garments like new rain, and maidens sprinkled with laughter and the scent of new womanhood, on their way to the marketplace behind the church.

The men came after them, with the sober demeanor of priests more than warriors. They no longer kept the village attire and their blue serge jackets over their short Indian trousers gave them the same grotesque nobility Chief Joseph had wearing a top hat over his feathers, as if defeat had also its own knighthood.

They carried fish, wooden furniture, and kindling wood, and fowl, and game meat of deer and wild pig. Two of the men, laughing like buffoons, carried a live iguana sketched on a pole, with her mouth sewn as if she would divulge a secret, and two green parrots the evangelists had given them. The parrots yelled from their cages, "Jesus loves you; Jesus loves you."

The water of my shower was cold and inflexible like the discipline of a Jesuit novitiate. Maria, the maid, had forgotten to light up my bath and was in the kitchen cooking chocolate and tamales with splendid odors of fresh banana leaves and cocoa nuts. She called the nuts *cacao*; that was the ancient name.

I wondered if there is any truth to what the Rogue said, about Michelangelo keeping his models nude in the cold until their organs shrank to the smallness required for his statues. The Rogue could not be trusted to be truthful, and the Professor suffered because of it.

But the water was cold, and its needles turned me into a model of chastity. Chastity would come in handy today; it was La China's birthday. I had been invited to her party, not that I meant to attend, but I had a present for her, a print of Manet, *Le Dejeuner sur l'Herbe*, where two fully-dressed gentlemen and a nude lady sedately converse about God knows what, while in the background another lovely woman, in a loose gown, attempts to catch fish or turtles in a creek. The original painting had caused quite an outcry at the Salon des Refuses. And, it is said, that when Napoleon III went by it, he asked Empress Eugenie to look somewhere else.

The print had arrived addressed to someone who had lived in my house years back, but Don Cosme had delivered it to me as the closest recipient. It came from a pharmaceutical company which advertised "Largactyl, the tranquilizer of excellence," written in gothic characters under the painting, suggesting that the detachment of the models was a result of their having been tranquilized.

Filomeno, the owner of La Rosita next door to my house, had promised to frame it in exchange for the plastic tubing with which he intended to build a periscope. He had left with the print and the casing, delighted with the bargain. I wondered what use he could have for a periscope in the landlocked village.

I went back to my window. The procession was gone, but the memories of it lingered. Memories always march at a slower pace.

"Maria, run to the street and buy the iguana the men are carrying!"

I heard her dash among a scramble of pots against tiles and the clanging protest of the street gate she threw open. She flew away like a falcon that had set course for a prey.

She was a *Tsutuhil*, Maria. Her people lived in Santiago, across the lake. They were defiant and proud, because they had never been conquered.

"They were gone," she said when she returned. "But they would not have sold it. If they did, what would be left for them to do at the market?"

"Will you be going?" I asked.

"We need so many things."

"What things?"

"Things for the house, *ocote* to start the fire, and wood to burn. Margarita burned all of your wood last night. She fell asleep by the fire and burned all of your wood. She left early in the morning. Said not to wake you. She will call, but had to leave for the city early. She said for me to buy more wood for when she returns."

"Did she say when she is coming back?"

"No, but she will return soon. She always does."

I hoped so. I never knew with Margarita; I don't believe she knew herself. I picked up two rocks. I was thinking about Filomeno's dog, Cisca. I never held him responsible for Cisca's manner, because it's the sad truth that there are ugly, mean dogs, which are that way from the very beginning. Even San Roque or San Francisco, patrons of animals as they are, couldn't tell me different. They themselves would've been in trouble trying to eulogize Cisca, because that bitch was born unredeemed, cruel and wicked. The only tranquil moment I had was when I thought she had died from eating a tin of spoiled mackerel.

But my weapon wasn't poison, nor could I kill a dog. Nor would Cisca, no matter how hungry, eat fish.

La Rosita was a tiny store made of a wood box the width of a man and his daughter with stretched arms. We had measured it that way. Rosita, the daughter, was eleven and had arranged the merchandise as she saw fit. Streamers of vivid green, yellow and deep blue hung from the beams, with strings of chorizo and cords of dried meat, and braided garlic and dried peppers like the ones seen in Santa Cruz. The shelves were crowded with red cans, alternating with blue and green ones, decorated with labels reminiscent of lottery cards, so that next to a hungry fish one saw tomatoes smiling at yellow suns and giants barely covered by green peas laughing happily as if all this vegetarianism was a joke. The counter was the center of temptation with jars of candy in the dangerous shapes of things that are delicious, honey-colored, purple and black, like licorice, with a flavor like opium.

The outside had been painted by a man known as Albino because his skin had no pigment and was transparent like that of a medusa. He worked only at night, to avoid the sun, and drew as his inspiration demanded, with the same insolent disregard for conventions that Diego Rivera had in his heyday. He had painted the front in blue, like the blue of the French flag, then in black Spencerian lettering, La Rosita, with a yellow daisy instead of a little rose, because he didn't like roses.

The shop was guarded by Cisca, who pretended to sleep but kept an eye open and a fang ready, dreaming of coyotes and snakes.

That was why I had picked up the rocks; she could guess whether I was armed or not. She pretended to be asleep if I was, but if I wasn't... Armageddon!

But Cisca was not there, and I dropped my stones, embarrassed. Without an enemy they were useless and heavy, like the revolver of El Capitan Lobo.

"A Nazareno passed by this morning, and she followed him," said Filomeno. "He called to her: '*Hotelucha*, won't you come with me?' And she went. She looked different, something about her face, as if she were laughing. Perhaps she was laughing at the name *Hotelucha*. There is no such name; he must have made it up, but she seemed to like it and went with him, without even looking back. I called her: Cisca, come here. Cisca, here. She didn't even look back.

"*El Nazareno* turned to me and smiled. He was a black man, dressed in loose white cotton trousers and a canvas blouse and wore an old beat-up, straw hat. He was barefoot. If the dogs hadn't followed him, I may have taken him for a fisherman who had come to buy lemons and salt, as they do. But the dogs followed...and that is how I figured his nature and knew he was a Nazareno.

"'Do you also want to come with us, Filomeno?'" he asked. But he was only teasing me. "'Bring me some *panela*, Filomeno,'" he said smiling.

"I felt I had to obey. I brought him a piece of the hard dark sugar, and he walked away gnawing little bits of it as if he were a squirrel. The dogs behind him were laughing. There were about seven of them following him, Cisca among them, looking happier than I had ever seen her.

"I became frightened because this was more like the workings of the devil. Jesus and the archangel San Miguel protect us, so I pulled the miraculous medal from my neck and bit the metal for protection against evil. The Nazareno turned and looked at me with great sadness. He made as if to speak but then just walked away with the dogs."

Filomeno went inside his house and brought my framed painting. Rosita had wrapped it in blue paper tied with a bright green and red ribbon.

Albino's art is rubbing off on her, I thought, and what about the Largactyl? Filomeno had framed my print in white pine, but had left intact the advertisement because he thought it was the name of the painting.

Does it really matter? asked the Professor. *What about the thousands who do not speak French; what do you think Le dejeuner sur l'herbe means to them? Or do you think they care that the young woman was Manet's most beloved model, Victorine Meurent? Do you think she looks like The Toreador? She is the same, and do you think she looks like Olympia?*

"I think La China does."

Yes, she does, said the Professor reflectively, *maybe Victorina came back to complete her karma.*

"And the Nazareno," I said. "What do you know about them? Why are they called by that name? Do they belong together with other Nazarenos, as monks do? Are they warlocks or witches? Do they travel alone?"

They are men, but different from other men, explained the Professor. *People call them Nazarenos, because of Jesus of Nazareth, yet that is only a name without meaning, because no one knows them. They come and then are gone, but dogs and birds and even animals from the wild follow them, bewitched with happiness and love. They are a mystery; that is what they are, a mystery perhaps, even to themselves.*

"I wish I could ask *Hotelucha,*" I said, and my voice was gentle.

Maybe if you rubbed your eyes with her tears you could see as dogs do, he said. *This is popular lore, you know—through their tears, one can see the ghosts they see.*

That was the main problem with the Professor, and for that matter with the Rogue. I never quite knew when they were mocking me.

VI

IGUANA

To see La China's happiness, one would've said I had given her an apple of solid gold instead of an Impressionist print. What would she have done had she seen the originals? Would she have ridiculed them like Louis Leroy, the critic; looked away like Louis Napoleon; treasured them like doctor Bellio, or Julian Tanguy; or bought them as charity to adorn a nest of illicit love like Gertrude Stein and Alice B. Toklas?

She kissed me clumsily almost with anguish, as children kiss when they are learning. The stickiness of her tears and saliva in my face felt warm and salty. I rubbed it off with my open hand. But when I saw her eyes wide with apprehension at the thought of having offended, I rubbed my eyes with her saliva and tears, in hope that I might see what she saw.

"The nude woman," she said, "who was she?"

"Her name was Victorine Meurend."

"Victorina?"

"That would be her Spanish name, but she was French."

"I lost my name somewhere," she said.

"You don't need a name," I replied.

Her hair once more covered her face like a veil, and her smile was again the smile of a temptress.

"I will tell you my name."

"Please don't!"

"I am Victorina," she laughed.

I felt relieved. We were playing our game. We would choose names from the stories I told her and then change the plots to make them better.

But it wasn't that easy. Not today it wasn't. I knew because I could see the same ghosts that she saw.

"Was Victorina... Did she work as I do?"

"She was a model for Manet, his favorite model."

"Do you think I look like her?"

"Yes."

"But I will never be a model. Will I ever be sitting with elegant gentlemen?"

"Never is a long time away. You could be a model like her."

"For Alizarin? He only paints volcanoes."

"No, not for Alizarin."

"Albino? He would make me look like a bat. Do you know what he painted for El Ultimo Recuerdo?"

Everybody knew. It was the scandal of the town.

"You can be Victorina, the model for Manet."

"And you and Alizarin are sitting with me in my garden. I have given you cheese from San Miguel and wine from Spain."

"Wine from Rioja."

"Yes, wine from Rioja. Now we are talking serious matters. Both of you are concerned about me and my life, and about Rolando."

"No, we are not talking about that. We are asking you to choose between us."

"I have already chosen, but will not say. There is never a profit in talking out problems of love." She paused, then continued. "But that is not what we are talking about either. I am embarrassed because I want to ask one of you to teach me to read," she said looking at me.

"I have wanted to ask you so many times, when you told me the stories but felt ashamed. But now, if I am going to be like Victorina, I have to learn."

She shook her head several times as if struggling to convince herself. I could never teach her, I thought. I couldn't look at her and think of words, and sounds. Nor would I like her trust. I could not teach her and want her, lest I be cursed by the gods.

She must have guessed my thoughts, because she smiled my favorite smile, half hidden behind her hair.

"You have been my teacher for a long time. You don't know it, but you already have been cursed. My friends here in the house and a man have cursed you, for taking me away. Now we must go on together."

She was only talking the sort of words she knew men liked to hear. But it was her birthday and it seemed an easy promise that I would teach her to read and not anything more.

I waited as always in the atrium of the Franciscan church. The fall harvest had been generous, and the *Cakchikel* had brought their offerings of maize, wheat and barley, and squash, sweet potatoes and yams, yuca and izote, aguacates and guavas and zapote, and sugar cane, and bags of black beans and red beans and beans with specks like the rump of an appaloosa, and chili peppers in all sorts of shapes and colors, red and orange and green so deep it seemed blue.

They had dug and planted wooden poles the height of a man standing on the shoulders of another, and tied ropes from one to the other, like the pentacles of the witches or the cross of the Christians. From the lines they hung their gifts to the church in a display of happy prosperity. They gathered the burlap bags of beans, the clay jars of honey and seeds, and placed them in small piles at the base of the poles.

Two men, dressed in the black and red ceremonial dress of *Cofrades*, sat by the church. One played a *chirimia*, a flute of sorts with only three shrill notes, while the other beat a long drum repeating the same monotonous beat forever, like the curse Dante wrote at the entrance of hell: "Abandon all hope, ye who enter here."

The Franciscan Church, pockmarked by *Churriguera*, presided with the confused demeanor of an old inquisitor attending a pagan ritual. Spanish soldiers had adorned its facade with baroque carvings of angels and cherubs with wings under their heads, saints with staffs like lances imploring curses and damnations over the infidels, and virgins throwing the hearts of sinners, who had desired them, into the flames of hell.

They had tattooed it, no doubt, as a soldier should, and it had helped in their conquest.

Don Cosme was serene, serious as an old bureaucratic file of the post office, with the precarious dignity of someone who doubts his principles even if he trusts his heart.

"Good afternoon, Quince; I am glad you came alone," he said.

"Alizarin must still be asleep," I said, "so I came alone."

"I am glad."

"Why are you glad, Don Cosme? Is there a letter?"

"No, not a letter, but there is a telegram."

"From where?"

"I don't know. Perhaps from the woman in Germany, the one he loves, and who never writes."

"What does it say?"

"I wouldn't know. It's in German. I asked the clerk to give it to me for delivery. Not legal, but I have it just the same. Take it now and give it to Alizarin, *cuando sea conveniente.*"

The yellow page with blue printing said: *Enfant etrangle par sa corde. Je ne t'aime plus.*

I counted the words. A child strangled at birth, and a love gone. One can say that in ten words. I kept the telegram in the back pocket of my trousers, where I kept things I wished to forget. I would deliver it when convenient.

Three o'clock is not a good time to walk at the *Cakchikel* market behind the church; the sun is still high. Flowers die early in the heat, and the smell of fermented fruits is like the smell of fear.

A young woman arranged her spring onions in neat rows like dominoes but wouldn't sell any even though the market was closing. She didn't want to spoil the symmetry.

The men with the iguana were drunk. The parrots were sold, and they refused to part with their last excuse to remain in the market. The tormented monster moved only in spasms, her mouth sewn by sharp little sticks. Her eyes, the terrible eyes of a small dragon in agony, were half covered by a gray veil that moved, each moment more slowly, like a hand trying to clean the pain of a horrific vision.

"Will you sell now?" I held a handful of silver coins and wrinkled bills.

"It is too early yet."

"But she may die."

"Iguanas don't die. They are cunning. They only pretend to die."

"How long since she drank water?"

"Iguanas don't drink water."

"How long since she ate?"

"I don't know." Then he turned to his younger companion. "Do you know when she ate?"

"Oh yes, she ate bananas and *aguacates*, and beans and hot chilies."

"And she ate *tortillas* and *pozole* and *chicharrones*."

They looked at each other and laughed and slapped each other's backs, and I laughed with them as if I had been infected by a fever.

"*Quieres a la iguana?*" the old man asked. "Do you have compassion for the iguana?"

He wasn't laughing. I didn't answer. I knew many men who spoke of Indians as these two men spoke of the iguana.

Then we noticed a soldier standing nearby. It was El Capitan Lobo. He looked at me and lifted a finger in friendly recognition. He was a handsome man with the easy manner of those who spend their lives in jungles or savannas and have learned stealth from rivers and tigers. His fatigue shirt was open at the neck, and he had a red bandana tied to it. That is the color of the government soldier. The guerrilla doesn't wear one. A simple kerchief separates the mortal enemies. Lobo wore his old revolver on the left side with the stock to the front. Like Wild Bill Hickok, I thought. The comparison amused me.

The two men stopped laughing, looked at him and then to me with apprehension, then averted their eyes.

"You can have her," said the older one to me.

"I will need a sack," I said.

The younger one brought a yute bag and slipped the iguana inside. Then he tied the opening and poured water on the bag, as I asked him to do.

"Now she will be refreshed, *fresca como una lechuga*!" he said, but the mirth was gone. Fresh as a lettuce and heavy, I thought, as I carried the sack over my shoulder. I waved farewell to *El Capitan*; he shook his head and smiled. I was glad he hadn't asked any questions. Maybe he didn't have to; *Capitanes* like him already know.

Burdened with the sack, I walked toward Helen's house several blocks down the hill.

Whoever had baptized Juan Domingo had earmarked him for glory, because he gave him two names, and that was unusual in a land where one name was enough and many times useless. Most men were called José and most women Maria, and that sufficed through their short anonymous lives.

Juan Domingo was El Guardian, the caretaker of Helen's house. He tended the garden and opened the gate. He also looked after Guacamaya, the macao painted with many colors, like an African flag, with the horrid beak that could crush a chestnut, and the noisy green parrots without names, Tigrillo the ocelot, and Zimba, a Rhodesian ridgeback.

He also cared for Cardamon, the male iguana to whom he fed hibiscus every morning, to bribe him so he would leave the vegetable garden alone. It had worked so far. Helen had her vegetables and Cardamon his hibiscus.

Juan Domingo took the bag from me.

"La Señora is away. Will be away for several days. Had to go to the border. Make yourself at home. Do you want something to drink?" he asked kindly.

"I'll have some coffee, but first look inside the bag. I'm afraid she may not live."

He took the iguana out holding her by the back of the neck. He had only one hand. He had lost the other somewhere in the fields from a snakebite. He had cut the bitten hand off with his machete before the poison could go far, and saved his own life. A *barba amarilla* it had been, as wicked a viper as there is.

He started to pull out the small wooden barbs which held the iguana's mouth sewn, using his own teeth as pliers. I stopped him and got them off using the tweezers of my Swiss army knife. The one with a thousand blades.

"Funny knife," he said laughing.

In an instant the iguana surged to life and sped off into the growth of the garden. Tigrillo, the brush cat, responded to the dare and scrambled after her. There followed a battle of claw and flailing tail. Suddenly, like a whip held in the air by an invisible arm, the tail flew off, flashing blindly. Tigrillo followed the wild lure that now wriggled in the dust in one last struggle, and lost his prey.

Juan Domingo, himself like a cat, had the iguana now by the back of the neck, avoiding the sharp claws that moved violently. She had lost her tail but was otherwise uninjured. He brought her now to a large cage with wood flooring and an old tree stump full of crevices to hide in and holes for water.

"This is Cardamon's old house," he explained. "She will be well there until she gets accustomed to the place." Then he brought her a head of watercress.

"There, he said, you are safe. Now grow strong."

He walked away to store some tools in the shed. I lingered.

The iguana came out of hiding and climbed the tree stump looking amusingly foreshortened. She fixed me in her black pupil. Slowly, she opened her mutilated mouth. And I affirm and swear...she spoke my name.

I caught up with Juan Domingo just outside of the orchard.

"Will her tail grow back?" I asked.

"It will grow good as new." He said. "Iguanas are luckier than men."

I looked at his missing hand.

Out in the patio, Tigrillo, the ocelot, sat watching the abandoned tail still uncomprehending. He started to wash himself.

Juan Domingo's wife, Manuela, had set a place for me under the arbor at a square table covered with a tablecloth of fabric from Nebaj, with simple embroidery representing houses, chickens and dogs and also bundles of wheat and fences made of corn stalks.

She had served coffee boiled with *panela*, and the shells of an egg, which was said to take away the bitterness. She served little tamales, *chuchitos de Chipilin*, made with rice dough and the leaves of a plant that had tranquilizing qualities; and *chuchitos de alfajor*, also tiny tamales but sweet and with a taste of anise. They were wrapped in corn husks and had the smell of clean country and kind life.

On one side she had set a glass and a bottle of clear rum but had not poured. This was an affair of men. I sat at the table. There was only one chair. Juan Domingo brought a stool and sat at the opposite end of the room,

~ 52 ~

not at the table, yet close to it, as if attending rather than partaking.

A Spaniard had planted his seed in brute land, and the germination had come to be Juan Domingo, a *criollo*, made of pride and truth, with blue eyes in brown skin like turquoise in a copper Maya mask.

"Juan Domingo, let me pour you some rum," I said and filled the glass.

As an actress waiting in the wings, Manuela appeared with another glass and set it in front of me.

"If it is your wish, I will," said Juan Domingo.

"I guess it is my wish, unless you are ill or *jurado*.

Being *jurado* meant that one had taken an oath in front of a crucifix in the presence of a priest to abstain from drinking for a determined time. One was given a yellow slip of paper on which the priest certified this to be true and warned anyone forcing drinks on the *jurado* that they would be guilty for his errors and sins while drunk. It was an offense among men to refuse a drink, and this offered the only way out.

"I am not *jurado* and my health is good," Juan Domingo said. "Will you drink with me?"

"I will, but only one drink, no offense meant; I have another place to go afterwards."

"No offense taken. I thought you may be *jurado*." He was smiling now.

I showed him my knife, blade by blade, and explained what each one was intended for. He found that amusing.

"We use our knives for only two purposes," he said smiling. "One is to cut bread or meat...the other..." He left his words trail.

"I couldn't use it," he said when I offered my knife to him. "But your offer is accepted just the same as if I had taken it."

He then offered me his own knife. It had been made from a steel file, ground to a sharp double-edged blade. The handle was made from the horn of a stag.

"The handle is the weak point," he explained. "It could break on a hard stroke. You must remember that."

Of course, I wouldn't take it!

He was loyal to his employer and was willing to give his life for her. It was easy to love Helen. She was born in Nevada and had arrived in the village with her gentle husband, a trumpet player. They never left. He had died from drinking, and she had carried on alone. It must not have been easy for her when she was young. Even now when, as she laughingly said, she was "eighty and eight," she still was a striking woman, dressed in a blue Hawaiian holomuu, which looked regal on her as she drove about in her pickup truck with her dog Zimba riding and growling on the flat back.

She had gone to the border to comply with the immigration law. Later, I found out, it hadn't been so.

It was a curious law. Every six months foreigners on temporary visas had to leave the country. They could re-enter on a new visa after spending three days away in a foreign country. Everyone spent the time in the closest town over the border. Twice a year, at every cafe, travelers discussed the merits of Tapachula or Comitan– the most popular border towns–before scattering like jacks thrown by a child. The immigration guards, friendly and kind, knew most travelers by first name and protected them from border mischief.

I, myself, was overdue for one of these journeys, and as luck may have it, as I was leaving Helen's house to go and seek Alizarin, down the road came Emilio Corzo, the jungle guide, driving his Land Rover, a spluttering beat up vehicle that looked as if it had been driven straight out of Africa.

VII

VISA

Emilio had known me when I was a child, before I left the region. His father, named Don Emilio, was a giant Spaniard from Navarra. Don Emilio had a white beard that reached down to his waist. He treated me as if I were one of his children. He had fourteen–I was the fifteenth–*quince* in Spanish. He pronounced it "keen-zeh" and since he called us by numbers, Quince became my name when I was among them. Emilio, my friend, was the oldest, and, as such, the only one entitled to a proper name. I however, called him "Uno," which in Spanish meant one.

The family lived by the lake, close to the volcanoes. Their house was immense and simple, mostly a row of rooms, like the cells in a monastery, to accommodate children and guests. It had a large kitchen with open fires where *Cakchikel* women, wearing their red *huipiles* and blue skirts, prepared great amounts of food. The household included not only family and friends but also Indian hunters–*Quiche*, *Tzutuhil* and *Chuj*–from the distant mountains of *Cuchumatanes*. The name *Cuchumatanes*, given to the distant high mountains, meant "land of the parrot hunters," but also "land of those joined by force."

We all ate together at a long table, on a large verandah adjacent to the kitchen. Don Emilio sat at the head with the women of the house, then came the guests and the children in order of birth, followed by the hunters, the *vaqueros*, and the farmers. At intervals, kneeling on the floor over a low fire with an earthen flat pan called a *comal*, a young Indian woman patted tortillas. We ate them hot, sprinkled with salt and chilies, and dipped them in soups made with turtle eggs, or wrapped them around bits of meat from the joints of steers that had been cooked on earthen pots over soft cinder fire until the meat fell off the bone. Then we had fowl, wild turkey roasted on spits over an open fire. There were also quail and wild dove in dark sauces made with garlic, onions, olive oil and wine, served on beds of white rice, and also deer, rabbit and hare, aged and seasoned by the hunters who knew herbs that grew without names in the fields and were unknown to others. The meal always ended with beans, delicious black beans softly boiled for hours in large earthen pots, with coriander, wild onions and a pungent herb called *apazote*, served soft and creamy with a slice of fresh cheese.

A young woman would bring the fruit, herself looking like the painting *Titian's Daughter Lavinia.* She carried a large basket with pineapple, guavas and mangoes. Also there was *pitaya*–a fruit of purple color with tiny black seeds as if invaded by mosquitoes– papaya, bananas, figs, oranges and slivers of sugar cane that abraded your teeth white as you bit into them.

Once in a while, a *montero*, a white hunter or prospector for *chicle*, would appear at meals, ragged by the hard life in the jungle and yellow-eyed with fevers, but rich with stories of emeralds in the sands of rivers or scribbled maps of secret places where the Maya had hidden gold.

They would look at the food like coyotes starved after a bad winter. Yet the *monteros* couldn't eat. Their shrunk and mistreated bellies were tight like angry fists. They suffered ugly cramps until their stomachs were soothed with teas of mint and chamomile. They were then fed soft broths, and little by little, over the days and nights, they regained their strength.

Don Emilio made his living trading skins of alligator and snake. The white-washed walls of the inner patio were almost covered by them nailed for drying. They looked like maps to me. I tried to imagine how those flat skins fitted the animals when they were alive.

In the yard, tied to stakes in the ground, were animals that had been trapped and were recovering. Some were being nursed because they were captured too young. There were deer with white fingerprints on their chocolate coats, ocelots licking wounded paws caught in steel traps, young ponies of many colors, hunting dogs, steers, fighting cocks, wild turkeys, geese and ducks. Also, birds and parrots. Cages made of wooden pegs, almost hiding brown *Tsenzontles* and jungle *Chiltotes* with orange breasts and a song so wild and loud that even the ocelots listened. The parrots made shrill whistle-like noises while they stood on one leg on their perches holding in their ugly claws bits of hard bread that they gnawed at incessantly. At times they listened with cocked heads to words they could never comprehend, reflecting perhaps, that to work so hard to learn so little, as Dickens' charity boy said at the end of the alphabet, was a matter of taste.

Those were now beautiful childhood memories. All of that is long gone. Emilio had become a guide for expeditions and a photographer for nature magazines.

He is a good guide who loves the land, the animals, and the plants. He knows the plants that cure and the ones that poison. For that he is said to be a healer, and some even call him *brujo*, a man who has secret deals with occult forces. But those are mostly rumors, whispers of envy from scared lips.

"I looked for you at your house, Quince," he said, over the noise of the Rover's engine. "I am going to the border early tomorrow. Cometh thee with me?"

"Counteth me in," I replied.

His archaic English was a private joke. Our nanny, Miss Zwikell, a Quaker, had taught us using the King James version of the Bible. To torment her, we used Spanish words and added 'eth' at the end. No one understood our English. Even as a child, however, when Uno was excited he spoke strangely with a lisp, and cursed with the gusto of a Melville harpooner.

He opened the passenger door. I climbed in and we drove to my house. Maria was waiting by the street gate.

"Am I glad you came!" she exclaimed. "The noises are impossible tonight! I shall leave early."

My house made strange noises at night, as if someone were throwing rocks on the roof. One could hear the shattering of glass or footsteps. No one worked for me at night, and even thieves never dared to break in. The house had a reputation as being haunted, but I never dispelled those rumors. Having a ghost in residence was better in Panimache than having the most alert dog.

The silver lining on a dark cloud, the Rogue would say.

I got my last bottle of Spanish brandy (it was Gran Duque D'Alva), and I gave it to Maria.

"Take this to Alizarin with this telegram. Tell him I will be away but will call him when I return."

"Alizarin?" she asked.

"Señor Alizarin, the French painter."

"Ah, the bread baker?"

"Yes."

"The one who lives across the wooden bridge?"

"Yes."

"I know him."

"Yes, you do; he comes often to visit."

"And I should take him the bottle and the telegram?"

"Yes."

Still, she didn't move.

"What do you guess the telegram says?" she asked shyly.

We started early, driving through the town that slept a lovely rest. It is easy to love a village when it sleeps.

We drove above the clouds and soon reached the highest plateau. From there we could see the silver water of the lake. We stopped to gape at the incandescence of the rising sun on the three volcanoes, which stood like oriental magi worshiping the birth of a god.

The road held the mountain gently.

A little behind us, across the road, we could hear the waterfall in the cove, where the women from Nebaj bathed to clean off the dust and sweat of their long trek, before entering the village. I had seen them often and thought of the *Bathers* by Cezanne, because they had the same rich freedom from malice as they frolicked under the cold water falling from the mountain.

I thought I heard soft laughter coming from the inlet. I saw a woman alone washing her long black hair. She wore a white *capixcay*, a short tunic that covered her body briefly as she moved in and out of the falling water, dancing to a melody only she could hear. She played with her hair, caressing it in her arms, then twisted it like a black rope over her breasts. She bent her head like a penitent, and kissed her red nipples alive with diamond droplets of water. She lifted her face and smiled at me. Slowly, her hair fell behind her back in abandon, but suddenly she twirled, and her beautiful hair covered her like a silk fan, and she let the cotton *capixcay* slide to her feet.

She beckoned to me as she walked slowly into the moss and umbra of the cove that opened behind the waterfall. I followed her, stepping carefully on the rocks, green like jade and gold and silver in the changing light. Then, blinded, I rushed in a reckless search of her nimble form lightly ahead of me.

Suddenly, I heard a gunshot and the metallic zing of a bullet that ricochets!

"Stop, you accursed fool!" Emilio yelled, grabbing my arm and dragging me back to the light outside the cove.

"Stop for your life!" he yelled again as I struggled to free myself. "She is *La Siguanawa*; she is a vampire! Look, you demented ass. Look where she is leading you!"

With his flashlight he lightened the path I was following. A few steps ahead, the beam fell on the horror of a hidden crevice. I saw her on the other side of the gap. She had parted her hair framing her breasts and was smiling as if saying, "There will be other times."

I knew she had led me toward destruction, and yet I felt anguish at leaving her. I followed Emilio back to the road, but slowly, staggering as a drunkard.

Emilio poured me strong coffee from his thermos bottle.

"Drink, Quince, even if it scalds your throat. You were very close to a horrible death."

"How did you know, Uno? Did you also see her?"

He was replacing the spent cartridge from his revolver.

"No, I only guessed. But I know *La Siguanawa* always appears close to the water where she washes her long hair as a lure. I saw you walk transfixed. I sensed she was calling you. Many men have died following her. And may God have compassion on their souls, because she is truly a demon leading Christians to perdition."

I felt exhausted and very sad. No matter what, it was not my way to believe evil of a woman. Perhaps they knew my weakness, the devils, for after all it is their business to know these things.

"Does she ever appear more than once?" I asked.

"Thou art mad," Uno said and started the engine of the Rover.

We could have driven forever–at least that is what Emilio said–but we stopped in Solola at a gasoline station where he got not only gasoline but also liquid gas; he had outfitted the Rover so it could burn one or the other.

"Isn't the gas flammable?" I asked.

"Yes, but isn't gasoline flammable also? In truth I tell, if we are going to worry about every little thing, we will die of apprehension. Have you seen Albino's painting in El Ultimo Recuerdo?"

He now was busy measuring his engine's oil with a bamboo branch as carefully as if he were taking the temperature of a patient with a thermometer.

"We can drive forever," he said, satisfied at the mark on the bamboo.

We drove on streets gnarled like the hands of old women; the town was old without having known the dissipation of youth. It transpired the self-righteous morals of someone who has never had a chance to sin.

"This town," Emilio said, "this town reminds me of a lovely spinster. It has everything going for her, and yet it wilts in aloneness."

"How would you translate *El Ultimo Recuerdo?*" he asked.

I tried several versions in my mind but none seemed to fit.

"Perhaps," I said: "The last thing to be remembered by."

"Not quite," he said. "How about: The last thing one can give as a remembrance?"

That was more accurate.

"It is a good name for a coffin shop," he said. "Don Moises, the owner, commissioned Albino to paint the outside. Albino painted a coffin but instead of the traditional two candles he painted two bottles, one of Heinz Ketchup, the other of Negrita Rum."

I didn't know what to think. The description was grotesque, even morbid. Yet, in some unique way, it fitted the carnival mood of the tragedy the land was now living. When we drove by, I saw the painting and was charmed. The blues, reds and greens merged in happy polychrome and negated the darkness evoked by the coffins.

Art offers a shortcut to knowledge beyond what reason can offer, said the Professor. *Don't try to understand or describe it; it is primeval.*

I knew better than to argue with the Professor. Albino's art had taken away death and replaced it with merriment–the joy of good drinks and company at the wake. Now people smiled and laughed as they went by.

If only Don Moises would give Albino a free hand decorating the coffins!

"Let me show you the prettiest cemetery in the world," Emilio said. We drove up the hill past a school where children in a circle were holding hands and singing as they moved. I recognized the song. It was about sneaking into a garden and watching a green frog eat parsley.

Solola's cemetery is unique. It is perched on a hill overlooking the valley, the lake and the volcanoes, suggesting eternity. The simple tombs are painted in pastel colors–yellow, blue and strawberry pink. The place looks like the patio of a kindergarten where the children have spilled their marbles and toys.

Uno held my hand and guided me; for an instant I thought we were in search of the green frog that ate parsley.

"Do you remember my brother Federico?"

"Federico?"

"We called him Siete, the seventh, he was the tallest..."

Now I remembered. Siete was tall and somewhat gangly, and he wrote poetry.

"Siete is here."

It was as simple a tombstone as any other, painted in sky blue. Uno was silent for a long time.

"I worried so much for Siete. He left our home and joined the guerrillas when he was only fourteen. He had read books about justice for the peasants, Russian stories by Andreyev, and Chekov; and he had heard of Che Guevara and of Tania. God knows what else he had read or heard, but he left and stayed away.

"One night two men came to my house to fetch me. They were guerrilla men, disguised as peasants. Siete was badly wounded and had called for me. It was a journey to reach him. On the way we had to dodge vigilante patrols armed by the government to kill on sight. When I arrived, Siete no longer recognized me. He thought I was a priest. He kept repeating, 'Forgive me Father for I have sinned.' I pretended to be a priest and he told me his confession. I have sinned more in one week than poor Siete had in his whole life. So I forgave him, in the name of Jesus, and made the sign of the cross on him, and after a while he died in peace.

"So now he is here. Can't tell a Spaniard from a *Quiche* or a *Tsutuhil*, can you? They all have about the same amount of land now and are all equally poor.

"You know Quince, this war is really a fool's game."

He looked away toward the mountains and volcanoes, then asked, "Do you suppose that his confession was valid and that God forgave his sins? Does it have to be a priest who absolves or can a man forgive another man?"

He shook his head and spoke to Siete's tomb.

"*Amigo*, dear brother, for both of our sakes, I hope God believed me and accepted my visa and that you are now in heaven."

VIII

EL CADEJO

The villages followed one another like pretty sisters on their way to school. We were in the highlands, and the fields were blond with wheat. Here and there, as if they had been planted in error by Albino, banana trees shivered. They looked like they could use a drink.

As we drove on, we heard the most beautiful sound a human can hear: the sound of a river as it rolled over boulders through the jungle. We breathed the aroma of jungle like the scent of a woman–not intense, but announcing its presence, brought even closer by the brief songs of birds and fleeting drops of color from butterflies.

Soon, the trees grew taller, and their branches held orchids like giants bringing flowers to women they loved.

I saw, flying over the green canopy of foliage, what seemed to be four gigantic birds with stretched wings, blue and green, yellow and red, circling slowly, descending toward the ground looking for a branch or a rock on which to alight.

We had entered the land of men who fly like birds.

"It is the dance of *el palo volador*," Emilio explained, "worth seeing even if we must deviate some from our route."

We drove into the small town and left the Rover on a cobbled side street, next to a tiny store that reminded me of La Rosita. I wondered what had finally happened to Cisca and the Nazareno. Then I noticed the large bushy black dog that had its red eyes fixed on me. Emilio had walked away and was already far along toward the plaza. A shiver that felt like the blade of a cold knife pierced my loins. I brought my hand to my throat where as a child a medal had protected me, but my neck was bare.

It is *El Cadejo,* I whispered to myself, the infernal hound that haunted my childhood. The dog sat as if waiting, his red eyes still on me in recognition. Then, slowly he got up and came to where I stood frozen, sniffed my legs and lifted his own to squirt his foul urine on me. Then he left.

I felt humiliated. Then my anger again turned to fear. My leg was dry, and, as the dog walked away, it cast no shadow.

Emilio waited for me at the plaza. He looked at me intently and shrugged his shoulders. "Maybe thou should be happy," he said. "Thou seemeth to be getting quite a homecoming from all the devils of the land."

"Was it *El Cadejo*?" I asked.

"What else?" said Uno. "What is unusual is that it came to you in daylight."

I wished to talk more, to ask questions and understand better. But that would have to wait. The spectacle before me in the plaza was so fantastic that it almost broke the boundary of reality. A straight pole, which was higher than the church's steeple, had been planted in the center of the plaza; a fragile platform at the top held four ropes, and from them, their feet held in loops, four men flew in a wide circle as in a magic spiral. They were dressed in feathers of brilliant colors, and their arms moved like the wings of birds as they slowly descended.

When they landed, each stood at a point of the horizon, east and west, north and south. The village elders dressed in short black jackets and black trousers reaching to their knees, held by a purple sash and with their heads covered by the ritual *tsutes*, approached them in respect to offer *aguardiente* and kernels of roasted maize.

It had been a ritual dance, *el palo volador*, the flying pole, or the "Dance of the Monkeys." The name was of no consequence; it was given only to describe the performance.

"Not much of a name," Uno said, "but perhaps this is how it should be. One could call them *Hombres Pajaros,* but that would make it circus-like, like the Flying Wallendas, the trapeze artists who would get shot out from a cannon and land on a net. This is totally different. This is an ancient ritual dance, perhaps from before the times of the seventh Nahuatl tribe. I don't know its meaning, and the very few who do know it won't reveal it to me."

"What do they fear?"

"Mysteries lose their power when they are divulged."

"But *El Cadejo* came to me in broad daylight!"

"No one can predict what *El Cadejo* does. He is a benign, infernal creature, which seems a contradiction. But Lucifer was an angel before he was thrown from heaven, and perhaps some of the good qualities stuck to him. Don't ask me difficult questions; theology was never my forte. The fact is: *El Cadejo* often protects drunks when they are lost at night or in danger of attack by robbers. He often came to play with you when you were a child, and he seemed happy today when he recognized you. Dogs, you know, mark with their urine what they regard as theirs."

"But is it then a dog?"

"Only in appearance, and even then he has the hooves of a goat."

Emilio became all at once preoccupied and restless like a cat prescient of an earthquake. He held my arm and walked me back toward the car.

"We must get out of here and make it straight to the border," he said in an urgent tone.

I didn't protest; I trusted Uno. I myself sensed the town had become alien and unfriendly as if it had caught a chill. Then, like a hiccup, came the ugly sound of automatic gunfire in short blasts, and the hurried anguish of villagers running for cover.

Soldiers quickly closed off the streets. They blocked the exits of the plaza and surrounded the church and the school building. The village people, in their colorful fiesta finery, milled into tightening circles. I thought of the agony of dolphins caught in a gill net.

The soldiers, indifferent to despair, separated the young men from the old, as if they were fish. It was the levy. The army needed recruits to continue its fight against the guerrillas.

Land Rovers always start when you really need them. *El Sargento* Feliciano Velada examined our papers and waved us away.

As we parted, I gave him the finger. It wasn't like me to do that, but he must have thought it was a good luck sign like V for victory.

IX

EL DUENDE

El Restaurante Yaxchilan was almost empty and had nothing to be remembered by, but it was across the border and out of danger's way. I looked at our food disconsolately. *Sopa de albondigas* was three pale balls of ancient beef floating in warm water, and the *mole de guajolote,* the well-known delicacy of turkey in a sauce of chocolate and four different varieties of pepper, had been insulted by a cook without respect for tradition or taste.

"This," I said to Uno, "reminds me of the Byron experience."

"It must have been some experience."

"Robert Byron, a descendent of Lord Byron, is an expert on icons and Byzantine art. It is his opinion that the true treasures of art in Greece are Byzantine, kept in the old Orthodox monasteries, and not the broken statues left by the ancient Greeks."

Emilio shook his head in mocking appreciation and poured more wine into my glass. "The point is," I continued, "that he set himself, sponsored by Oxford, to photograph those treasures. He visited very old and forgotten monasteries. To me it was terrifying to read how the monks lived, and that there are still Orthodox monks, but that is not my point."

"It is interesting nonetheless," Uno said sincerely.

"Not once, in any of the monasteries he visited, was he served a decent meal."

"Why should it be different?"

"By tradition, monasteries should be well provided with great food. I myself have had some of my best meals while being a guest of the Benedictines."

"I had a terrible meal at the Benedictines once," Uno said.

"Was it Father Michael's turn to cook?" I asked.

"As a matter of fact, it was."

"You must try some other time."

"Isn't it irreverent to go there for a meal?"

"Not at all. In fact I am told by a Buddhist devotee that in Singapore she would often go to Theravada, a temple of the Small Wheel, for gourmet vegetarian food, because the monks have secrets of cooking unknown to others."

Surprised, we heard the sudden laughter of youth. We turned to meet the bright eyes of a young American woman.

"Didn't mean to intrude," she said, still laughing. "I overheard you; I sure could use some vegetarian recipes. Tommy would be delighted. Or at least, if worse came to worse, I could send him to the Theravada."

"Are you a vegetarian?" I asked.

"Not this kid. Tommy, my husband, is. And believe you me, cooking for him isn't an easy task."

I looked for Tommy but saw no such American husband.

"He's out in town, changing the oil and outfitting the camper. I'm Mary," she said, extending her hand to me and then to Emilio. "We're on our way to Tikal and then south to the lake in Solola. We drove all the way from Ashland in southern Oregon."

I knew Ashland, the theater town, home of the Shakespearean festival, a lovely small community with picturesque old homes overlooking the rolling Siskiyou and the Cascades.

"Is the North Light still there?" I asked. "That is a vegetarian restaurant."

"The only one, as a matter of fact" she said surprised. "Yes, it's still there."

"And the Key of C?"

"Same, but that's a bagel and coffee house now."

"It always was."

A good town, Ashland. I had often thought it was the best place I had known for children to grow up in, and where men could grow old.

Mary was an environmental lawyer. She had worked with the Peace Corps during the sixties and loved the land and the Maya, whose life she had shared.

"Tommy and I hope to adopt a native child," she said. "That's one of the reasons for our trip; I also wanted him to see where I worked when I was young."

Mary was slim and tanned. Her smile made me think of peppermint. She had brown eyes, near-sighted eyes, and her glasses kept sliding down her nose. She was very pretty. She was dressed in a loose blouse with stripes, baggy Dockers and deck shoes.

"Why don't we just forget about eating here and build a cookout together?" she asked. And that is what we did.

Tommy was worthy of her. We learned he had played hockey in college long enough to realize his vocation would not be scholarly. And, with the enviable sincerity of those who can afford it, he had learned a trade. He was now a carpenter, a cabinet maker. He had inherited land in Oregon and bred quarter horses. He and Mary lived on the farm not far from Ashland.

The evening ended around a campfire where Uno roasted a fat goose brought to him by a man who wanted his advice. Tommy roasted potatoes and turnips wrapped in corn husks and kernels of maize that the man had brought. The man had arrived earlier and had helped set the camper's tent. He had started the fire. He was in his forties–rugged forties–tanned by tropical sun and rain and wind. His name was also Emilio, like Uno, and this created much confusion, so he told us his second name, José, and we called him Emilio José. A good feeling spread because few things bring men closer together than to be called by their names.

He spoke directly.

"I didn't mean to share this with all of you. But I have changed my mind because you seem fair and honest people who wouldn't make fun of me. Not that I would permit it, nor would my friend Emilio nor Quince, whom I knew as a child. I say this because it is easy to make fun of certain things.

"Well, I am a cattleman and own a few head here in lands that used to be of the Dominguez in Comitan. They should've stayed here, the Dominguez, but they went south. Every man I guess must follow his own voices.

"Now let me explain. I own some good cattle, Cebu and Brahma, and I am kept busy looking after them. I am married and have a nice family. This is where the problem is. My oldest girl, around seventeen–just turned into a woman–has fallen in love with the *Tzitzimite*. That is one of his names; others call him *Tzipitio*.

"Maybe she took after her mother, but her looks remind me of an aunt on my maternal side. She has long black hair and large soulful brown eyes, and it is not for me to say it because I am her father, but she is a beautiful woman.

"Joséfina, that is her name, although I call her Pepita, started complaining that at night a little man would keep her awake, singing and dancing. She described him as being about the size of my hand, dressed in a short black jacket and tight trousers, fastened by a silver belt. He wore high-heel boots and a large hat, like a Mexican sombrero, that hid his face, except for his long black mustache. He courted her with sweet words and sang doleful love songs. At other times he danced with so much grace that, in spite of herself, she was charmed.

"We thought she was dreaming about it or imagining things. You remember, Emilio, how your sister Clarita had that imaginary friend she called Lanika?"

"I remember," Emilio said, "but this sounds different."

"Unfortunately it is. The story gets worse. Little by little, Joséfina changed in her feelings toward Manuelito, which he told her was his name. She spent her nights waiting for him to serenade her. At other times he would braid her hair in tiny knots that could not be undone and had to be cut. He would carry the hair snippets away as tokens of her love and asked her to make a little pillow with them for him to keep.

"She was losing weight and not sleeping, and soon she hardly ate because, she said, Manuelito would throw dirt in her food. We were at a loss; my lovely Pepita was turning into a sad sight. I set mouse traps and spent hours by her bedside with a fly swatter but he wouldn't come when I was there. Instead, he would go and frighten my horses, braiding their manes into tiny knots. After a week of this, all of my horses had to have their manes cut off because it was impossible to undo the knots, and what was worse, they became skittish by the experience and were never the same as before.

"I wish you had been here, Emilio, but it's better late than never. I have sent Joséfina to my sister's home in Xelaju, were they tell me at least she is eating better but spends her time sewing little pillows filled with her hair for Manuelito. Meanwhile, this little bastard must be furious at me for sending her away and has started tormenting my cattle, frightening the cows to where their milk turns sour.

"I have hoped that you, Emilio, might be able to help, and that is why I called you."

"I believe I can," Uno said, serious and intense.

"It is the *Tzitzimite*," he said. "*El Duende*, as some call him, one of the spirits of the land. Manuelito, which is one of his names, has a weakness for young women with black hair and brown eyes like Pepita. He is mischievous and a pest but not evil in the true sense. Tomorrow we must get a table made of unpainted pine, also a little silver guitar."

He turned to Emilio José.

"Do you think you can get that?"

"Count on it, even if I have to make it myself."

"I can help," Tommy said.

"At nightfall you must place the table under an apple tree and the silver guitar on it. Then you must say aloud: '*Tzitzimite*, you may have Joséfina only if you can sing for her the songs that they sing in heaven.' You must say this three times, at sunset, at ten, and at midnight.

"And what will happen?" Mary asked.

"You'll see, Mary, you will see," Uno smiled.

It was early in the morning when we gathered again. The night had been balmy and restful, and it was lovely to awake to the smell of fresh coffee brewing and the fragrance of flowers.

The birds sang too loudly for my taste; I prefer other sounds, the sound of young pigs feeding on wooden troughs or cows munching grain, or the sound of horse hooves on cobblestones or leaves swept by a light breeze. The tropics have many ways to speak of freedom and warmth!

Emilio and I had been guests of Emilio José at his home in town. A simple house of large whitewashed rooms that opened onto a central garden. My window opened to the back patio, and I could smell the fresh hay from the horse stalls and hear them talking at night.

A table had been set at the verandah on the central garden and was alive with steaming pots of fresh coffee. Two horses had been saddled, western style, and waited outside the house, tied to the window bars. They were horses for Mary and me; we were to ride to San Cristobal and find the little silver guitar. Tommy would help Emilio José build the pine table.

"I'll also be busy, one way or another," Uno said.

We drank big mugs of coffee, sweetened with brown sugar, and ate fresh baked bread with honey. Then Mary and I left, our horses playing castanets on the loose stones of the street. It always happens when a man and a woman ride together in open country that they become enamored and can guess what the other is thinking. This is one of the mysteries that even the Professor could not explain.

The Professor had become very active, analyzing what was happening. *Go on,* he would say, *look for your little guitar to cure Pepita. She suffers from dementia praecox; can't you see everything fits? Her age, that is when the illness strikes, and her lack of sleep? And playing with her hair? And laughing to herself, and now not eating?*

"Is she ill?" Mary asked as if she had heard my inner thoughts.

"She is heartsick," I said.

"But why?"

"Part of her is dying, and this always hurts."

"Do you mean the child in her is going away?"

"Yes, that is what I mean."

Mary was silent. Tears formed in her eyes.

"Come away, O human child," she said softly. "For the world's more full of weeping than you can understand."

She had said a few lines of "The Stolen Child," the poem by Yeats, in which happy fairies lure a child away into their world.

"I wonder," she said, "if we, Tommy and I, are doing a good thing taking a child from here to bring him up among us. Oh sure, we have been approved as fit parents, and our life, or at least the life we can offer, seems much healthier to a growing infant. But what will be best in the end? Are we robbing from him his rich heritage?"

"We will need to ask Emilio," I said. "Perhaps he knows an enchantment to dissipate gloomy thoughts. The fairies in the poem had none of these remonstrations. Perhaps you are not a true fairy Mary; maybe you only look like one."

I was glad Mary knew the country and the language and the values that prevailed, for it spared me the vexation of shopping for a tiny silver guitar in a town where a man could buy fishing tackle or powder or guns or grain or saddles, but little more.

Besides, in the whole town of San Cristobal, there were no silver guitars of any size. Not in the music shop nor in the marketplace nor at the Chinese shop where one could find everything else, not even at the antique shop; and yet it was there, at *El Recuerdo de la Tia,* something which I loosely translated as The Aunt's Souvenir, that Mary noticed a bibelot of Colombine being serenaded by Pierrot. He was holding a silver mandolin.

I still have the piece. It was made in Italy. Mary gave it to me after snapping the mandolin out of Pierrot's hands.

"There," she said. "He is much better off without courting this hussy anyhow."

Maybe she didn't mean it that way, but I became shy and didn't flirt with her anymore. I told her about my life in the village and about my sailing in *El Termometro Feliz,* my sloop, and I promised her we would sail together and visit the twelve islands in the lake, named after the twelve apostles. We enjoyed each other's company as we rode back, hoping that Manuelito knew how to play the mandolin.

Emilio said that the pomarosa tree would do as well as an apple tree, and that was a relief because apples do not grow in the tropics. Poma, a small aromatic fruit, is the apple of the jungle, and there was one such tree outside of Pepita's old room.

We had missed the first intonation of the enchantment at sunset and now eagerly awaited the darkness of the early night.

The moon was at its growing quarter.

"About the same age as Pepita," I said.

Mary held my hand for an instant, and her tender gesture sent a glow of delight so intense that I feared I had lit up like a firebug and imagined everybody's eyes were on me.

It wasn't so. Everyone–Emilio José and Tommy, Emilio, and Emilio José's wife Doña Eufrasia–were attentive only to the pine table under the tree, with the little silver mandolin on it.

"Now," Uno said in a whisper.

Emilio José stood up. "Manuelito, can you hear me? You may have Joséfina if you sing for her the songs they sing in Heaven."

There was silence for a moment; then we heard the silvery cords of the mandolin and then, soft sobbing, a gentle cry, so desperate, hopeless and tormented that all of us cried with Manuelito for the lost loves in our lives.

X

RETURN

It was providential for me that Father Michael Cassidy, S.J., from Newman Center, in Honolulu, Hawaii, as he had carefully written on the first page, had forgotten his Jerusalem Bible at the hotel room were we stayed for one night in Xelaju. I had been four days without reading and felt as empty and restless as an insomniac.

Unknown to her, a daughter keeps her father awake,
the worry she gives him drives away his sleep:
in her youth, in case she never marries,
married, in case she should be disliked,
as a virgin, in case she should be defiled
and found with child in her father's house,
having a husband, in case she goes astray,
married, in case she should be barren.

According to the *Ecclesiasticus*, Emilio José had many sleepless nights ahead of him due to his concern for his daughter Pepita. The Bible was not a cheerful book, and when it came to bringing up young women, it was woefully dated.

We were on our way back home, which after a long trip always feels like sliding on a toboggan, but we stopped to visit with Pepita in Xelaju, the town with a name that sounds like the mating call of a bird: "Shel-ah-hoo." I wondered whether our incantations had been effective and feared finding her still sewing pillows for Manuelito. We saw her, but only briefly. As if invited by a mysterious scent, many young people had joined her, and gathered long-legged and chirping like a flock of curlews. She looked pert and happy on her way with them to a band concert in the park, waving farewell to us, delighted with her new-found freedom and without regret for ghosts with broken hearts.

I remembered as a young man also going to concerts in the park. The military band played marches and polkas at a central pavilion while we men circled in one direction and the women in the opposite one so that we met twice every circle for a glance of recognition. It was almost impossible to stroll casually when the rhythm of the music demanded that one marched. It was a wonder that so many courtships, which started by such martial and brief encounters, ended up in marriages.

Emilio was silent as we drove off. He took some side streets until we reached the park. We could hear a loud twanging of guitars a couple of blocks away. On the grass surrounding a stage, young people had set their mats and reclined with the abandon of intoxicated Bedouins. On the stage a young man wearing torn jeans seemed intent on swallowing a microphone as he sang. The noise was horrendous, and I wished to escape, but Uno held my arm. So I waited. Very soon, as if transfixed by magic, the same singer intoned ballads of beauty so intense that tears came to my eyes as naturally as drops of rain.

"What was your youth like?" I asked Uno.

"I didn't notice it," he said dryly.

When we drove off, he was sad. We had no radio in the old Rover. I wished to change his mood, so I opened my stolen Bible at random, and once more, as if following the amusing instructions of Father Michael Cassidy, S.J., it opened at Ecclesiastics in the Apocrypha.

"Tell me, Uno," I said, "do you heave bitter sighs when you go out to dinner with your neighbors? And have you slack hands and sagging knees?"

"Now, where did you get that idea?" Uno asked laughing.

"Ecclesiasticus, 25:3. Those are two of the indications a wife is making her husband wretched."

There is no poison worse than the poison of a snake,
there is no fury worse than the fury of an enemy.
I would sooner keep house with a lion or a dragon
than keep house with a spiteful wife.

"Do you have those problems Uno?" I asked, looking into his brown eyes as he stared at the road ahead.

No such danger, I thought. He had a lovely wife. She had been also a lovely woman, but through years of maternity and village life, she had become heavy, firm and unbending.

"Carmen, my wife, and her new friends, the *feministas furiosas*, as I call them behind their backs, would burn your book, and maybe also burn you with it," said Uno. "Sometimes I wish they would simply burn us all to ashes and give us peace! When they band together in a frenzy, they are worse than a pride of lions and a hundred dragons!"

Uno was an old hand at heaving bitter sighs.

"It would be only fair," I said. "Not so long ago men burned women for daring to think, and it was a sin for women to be educated. This book was written in a land where even recently women were not permitted to eat at the same table with men. And yet, paradoxically, from the same book, listen to this:

> 'The grace of a wife will charm her husband,
> her accomplishments will make him the stronger.
> A silent wife is a gift from the Lord,
> no price can be put on a well-trained character.
> A modest wife is a boon twice over,
> a chaste character cannot be weighed on scales.
> Like the sun rising over the mountains of the Lord
> is the beauty of a good wife in a well-kept house.
> Like the lamp shining on the sacred lampstand
> is a beautiful face on a well-proportioned body.
> Like golden pillars on a silver base
> are shapely legs on firm set heels'."

"Whoever wrote that," Uno said, "was a good politician."

I always marveled at the charm of the village. When seen from high up in the mountain, it reminded me of an Indian maiden washing her feet in the waters of the lake. If only there were no soldiers. But this was not to be. While we were away, there had been a failed coup against the president who had retaliated with a campaign of repression. The civilian militia had been mobilized, and as we drove, we encountered small groups of armed peasants marching behind a flag carried precariously on a bamboo staff. They were not soldiers but *Cakchikel* peasants who had been separated from their brothers and drafted into the government militia; in their confusion they aimed to convince the military authorities of their loyalty, exaggerating their zeal.

They searched the farmers for weapons on their way to work in the fields and opened their *ixtacates*, the small bundles in which they carried their tortillas and beans and chilies for the noon meal, in case they brought more than needed to share with men from the guerrillas. The *Tzutuhil* protested this humiliation. Their pride was not respected but regarded as defiance. This led to the massacre of Santiago which happened some time later during a sun eclipse, which Juan Sisay, the *Tsutuhil* artist, who was one of the victims, had painted as a bat devouring the sun.

We entered the village and breathed its aroma and once more became intoxicated as if we had inhaled opium. I recognized the dogs which barked at us with little interest, mostly out of habit: Cuta, owned by Niña Joséfa, the woman who delivered bread, carrying an immense basket on her head; Chica and Patroclo, the pharmacist's dogs, always asleep in front of the pharmacy, as if sedated by the smell of disinfectants; and the butcher's fat and sassy dogs Chilindrina, Kako and Pericles.

As we drove by the church, I saw Alizarin entering La Oficina de Correos, and remembered the telegram. I asked Uno to let me off.

"Thou could drop my bag at my house and wait for me; we could have dinner together," I said.

"Suits me fine," Uno said. "I saw smoke coming off thy home's chimney as we drove down toward the village. This means Margarita is at thy house."

I would trust Uno with my life, yet I wished he went to his own home and to his own *furioso* woman instead of going to Margarita. Uno had a way with women, no two ways about that.

I decided to wait in the church. A wooden image of Saint Francis of Assisi, the *poverello*, presided over a congregation of dogs and a man who wrung his hands and beat his chest in front of the saint, as if trying to convince him of the firmness of his repentance. I recognized Jacinto, the drunken plumber. He always repented when he ran out of money. He belonged to the Alcoholics Anonymous group that met at the church. He never went sober more than four days, and of their twelve steps to rehabilitation–which he had carefully explained to me, while digging useless trenches in my garden to find a buried treasure to explain the "haunting noises"–he only accomplished the first, which was to publicly admit he was an alcoholic, something everyone in the village knew anyway. I avoided looking at him. I didn't feel comfortable to be seen in the church, as if I were trespassing. My own patron saint was also a Franciscan, Saint Francis of Paula, but a misunderstanding had separated us.

Traditionally, as soon as a child can walk, he is brought to the church to meet his patron saint, and so it was done with me. To my misfortune, however, as I bent to kiss my saint's sandal, his walking staff fell off his hand and clobbered me on the head. Nothing serious, although it required stitches, but my grandfather, who was also my godfather, interpreted it as a personal affront, and in spite of the efforts of the priest, Don Bruno, who explained that my saint was selecting me for especial tasks, my grandfather forbade everyone in the family from associating with that saint.

So, I grew up without a patron saint and even had to give up the name Francisco, and pray to borrowed saints.

Jacinto's repentance did not bring immediate reward. He became violently sick while the dogs watched with interest. As I left, I dropped a few bills where he could find them after wrinkling them so they would look illegitimate and used. Crisp bills will never do when one is trying to be incognito and give the credit to a saint.

Alizarin was leaving the post office as I came out of the church. He smiled the ironic smile that Frenchmen have inherited from centuries of mastering misfortune with poise and dignity.

"You heard of course the bad news?" he asked.

"The telegram?" I asked.

He nodded.

"Thank you for the brandy," he said. "Almost as good as French cognac."

"The Spaniards think it's better."

"The Spaniards will never learn to take their wines seriously," he said. "*Quieres un café?*"

"Are we going to *Al Chisme*, where we got shot at?" I asked.

"This time we should go to *El Psychodelico*," he said. "It has a beautiful staircase, which is going to waste, because the owner doesn't know how unusual it is."

It was a stone staircase, simple, but firm and meaningful, with short steps even Indian women could take restricted by their tight *cortes*, the skirts that keep them bound in a cocoon. It reclined on a whitewashed wall and it went nowhere; the upper floor was never completed.

"It is a beautiful staircase," I said, "yet I can't explain its charm."

"Neither can I," Alizarin said, "but it is very much like life–one cannot take two steps at a time."

We drank our coffee in silence. I examined the staircase; one could take two or even three steps at a time, but only if one wished to reach the end sooner. Alizarin was talking in metaphors or perhaps he lived a life of metaphor. Painters do that. Their canvases are nothing but symbols of their visions.

"*Est-ce que tu est...*" Alizarin started to ask.

"No." I wasn't sure what he meant to ask.

"The telegram, *tu sabes*? It was only a horrible subterfuge of my woman's mother to disillusion me. It succeeded. I was in despair until I understood her diabolical intention."

"And now that you have understood?"

"I will wait for a letter of explanation. It should be forthcoming."

I was about to protest. His disregard of reality was almost a provocation, but a look at the staircase soothed my indignation. I remembered he could only take a step at the time, and, in any event, the staircase led nowhere.

A man walked by in the street, carrying on a small cart a vat filled with live crab and shrimp and two large black bass. Alizarin called him and went to inspect the fish, looking carefully inside their mouths.

"It is the eyes you wish to look at," I said, "to check for freshness."

"One can tell at a glance they are just out of the water," Alizarin said. "I was looking for a gold coin."

"A gold coin?"

"Tobias found one in the mouth of a fish." He spoke with conviction, as if the Biblical character lived next door. Besides he had the story wrong. I paid the fisherman who left with his struggling crabs.

"We could take the fish to your house, and I will prepare dinner."

"Uno will be there," I said.

"Great, it will be like a family reunion!"

"Did you find a gold coin?"

"Of course not," he said. "If I had found one, I would have told you at once!"

He must have been doing fine paintings if he was so poor as to search for gold in the mouths of dead fish. Maybe his bread was not selling, or he wasn't baking at all. His art and his cooking alternated. It was easy to guess the condition of his work. His bread was abundant when he was not creating. But when he painted his best canvases, it was famine!

I called Pedrito, the boy who cleaned the café tables, and asked him to take the fish to my house.

Alizarin and I walked slowly through alleys and small streets to avoid the bicycles that buzzed in the early darkness, blind and clumsy like June bugs. Back streets have their own charm. The houses, small and square like dice rolled on the dust, had no windows, and the doors, always open, were guarded by old men dressed in black jackets, with buttoned-up white shirts without ties and wearing black hats which they removed to wish the passersby a fine evening. What did they wait for, sitting alone on their sturdy chairs?

"Que esperas?" I asked. The sound of my own voice was hollow.

The old man smiled like an old cobra; maybe my asking was only to torment him.

I saw my house and felt grateful that it was there waiting like a trusted friend. The red gate was not locked. The lights were on, revealing the disarray of worn out curtains billowing from open second story windows like the skirts of witches in flight. No wonder my house, even without the noises, had such a reputation as a haunted place.

The front door opened before I even knocked. It was Margarita who opened it. As I saw her, I couldn't contain a gasp of surprise.

Margarita had become a boy.

XI

ROLANDO

*Home is the place where
if you have to go there
they have to take you in.*

I was reminded of the Robert Frost lines as I followed Margarita while trying to master my surprise. Gone was her beautiful auburn hair. Her head was completely bald as if a tornado had mowed her braids off, as happened once to a farming girl in Olathe, Kansas. But in the back Margarita had left a long tuft, like a Tartar.

She was wearing black, tight jeans and a white blouse, with loose sleeves. Her boots stood at attention by the fireplace that glowed with the fury of a locomotive furnace, and on the table her black astrakhan hat lay misshapen as if worn by a reveling Cossack.

I thought of Armanda, the heroine of Hesse's *Steppenwolf* who appeared both as a seductive woman and as a charming young man, sexually confusing the already bewildered hero, and like him, I was caught in the contradiction of my sensual attraction for a woman who now looked like a boy. My thoughts fluttered from guilt to anguish.

I hoped Uno could explain. Margarita saw me glancing about and smiled.

"Uno is not here," she said smiling. "I sent him home. Alizarin has gone straight to the kitchen. A child brought the fish that you sent."

She then came to where I was and kissed me. Her lips parted on mine and her hand held my hair as I used to hold hers, and I was no longer afraid.

"I am happy that you are back and that I am back," she said. "We shouldn't go away from each other."

"Did you shave your hair to torment me?"

"They shaved it at Scott and White, the clinic in Temple, but they left the tuft to humor me. Helen had a neurologist friend visiting her, and they flew me with them for tests. He thought surgery could help with my condition. That's what he called my moments of absence. They shaved my hair and with small needles recorded the depths of my brain. Surgery won't help."

I held her close to me. Love and tenderness can flow from a man to a woman with the easy grace of clouds that change forms without concern for meaning. I loved her in many ways that no words could express.

"Will you love me even when I am away?" she asked.

"Have I not loved you?"

"But now you know how it will always be. I will be absent for moments, sometimes those instants will turn into pauses and you will wonder when they will end. Will you be there waiting for me when I return? Can you share me with the gods that call me away?"

I wish I had been more affirmative then, when she needed for me to be.

"I guess so," I replied.

"You'd better guess right," she said and laughed and kissed me again. Then we both went to the kitchen to find out what Alizarin was doing with the fish.

I thought I heard a child's cry, but I couldn't be sure. It was always so with the noises in my house.

Alizarin had set the kitchen table with frivolity and humor. From an empty bottle of wine sprang two or three spring onions, their heads carved in the shape of orchids. In the middle of the table lay a purple cabbage opened like an exotic rose with colorful toothpicks offering bits of yellow cheese. He had baked the fish with fresh butter and deboned it, then set it back together in a large pale blue platter adorned with strips of green lettuce and seaweed.

The table was brightened by five candles, each a different color: mauve, green, blue, white, and black. Alizarin had gone to the cellar and now triumphantly decanted a bottle of Clos de Vougeot 1968.

"A Burgundy with fish?" Margarita asked.

"A fine wine honors any meal," Alizarin said. "Besides, the black bass is a game fish. Someone introduced it into the lake hoping to improve the fishing. The bass promptly devoured the existing native species; now most Indian fishermen must cultivate vegetables or hire out as journeymen to eke out a living since the fish they had been catching for centuries with their scanning butterfly nets are gone. Now the bass are eating the ducklings of the Pock, an endangered native diving duck that fed on the lake's small fish."

"My heart goes to the native fisherman," I said. It seemed to be the thing to say—entropy leaves no room for comments. For all his atrocities, the big fish was excellent to eat.

"It is no way to live," said Margarita, "to be a duck on the verge of extinction."

She looked at me maliciously, and I felt alluded to. She seemed giddy like a schoolgirl trying to keep a secret. She and Alizarin averted looking at each other, like accomplices do, in soap operas.

"This lake," she said, "attracts all sorts of forces and errors. It is a site of power."

Now, I thought, after this prologue, I should brace myself to hear some confession. But it had been a very long day, and the beautiful wine and meal and the warmth of the fire sedated me into a quiet sleep that sneaked in on tiptoes.

I woke up to the sound of a child crying. I was alone in the kitchen, but the table had been cleared. In the living room the fireplace nursed cinders in soft white ashes. I must have slept long, I reflected. Then, again I heard the cry of a child. It came from my bedroom, and, as I walked up the stairs in the tenuous light, I also heard the voice of Margarita singing softly.

She was sitting on my bed wearing one of my sleeping gowns and a night cap; in the soft light of a Coleman lantern she looked bewitching. My attention was arrested by the child she was holding and stroking softly.

"It is Rolando." She formed the words without sound.

Calmed by her song, the child slept, and she placed him in a wooden box arranged with soft pillows and covers like a rabbit's nest. She walked ahead of me toward the fireplace, and there, in front of the gentle glow, we sat. She should have always walked barefoot; she had the prettiest feet I had ever seen on a woman.

"It is Rolando, La China's child. She's in jail and she asked that the child be brought here to his father's care."

"His father's care," I uttered, perplexed. "Who is his father?"

"You are. She feared they would take the child away to the orphanage, or worse, that one of the women in the house would claim him. She pleaded with me to ask your forgiveness because she signed a legal paper saying that you are the child's father, which gives you the right to protect him."

"What has she done?"

"She attacked a soldier, Felipe, the friend of Lobo. She slashed his face with a broken bottle. It happened the day you left," Margarita continued. She seemed amused, but no, it was only the lovely curve of her lips that always gave her an amused expression.

"It was her birthday, and she gave a party."

"I know; I was invited."

"It must have been some party. Alizarin attended; he told me what happened. Half the regiment was there."

"La China sang and danced by herself on the stage and asked to make a speech. She announced that soon she would be leaving to join her aunt Victorina who lived in Paris and was the favorite model of the famous artist Señor Manet. She had a copy of his last painting with her aunt Victorina posing."

"Alizarin then unveiled *Le dejeuner sur l'herbe*, which was hanging on the wall behind the stage. Everyone applauded and yelled that they could see the family resemblance."

"Do you think she looks like the model?" Margarita asked.

"I often thought so."

"The party went on. Cider was served, and La China went happily from group to group like a debutante, basking in new fame and respect. But the devil never rests. Felipe was drunk and envious of the attention. So with a piece of charcoal, he painted a phallus on Victorina. La China was the last one to notice when the soldiers laughed obscenely. She screamed a terrible scream and slashed Felipe's face with a broken bottle.

"She has been in jail since but was given permission to speak with a friend. I was surprised that she asked to talk to me and tell me about the child. I didn't know her, but she knew my closeness to you."

And that is how Rolando entered my life without asking permission, like children do when they crawl on your lap and you haven't the heart to shove them away.

Seven days went by, maybe longer, it isn't easy to keep count when you are happy.

Maria, the *Tzutuhil* woman helper in my house, responded now to the name Elisabeth. She had been baptized by immersion in the lake by the evangelical missionaries and given her new name.

The missionaries had a new enticement for conversion; it was an album of photographs of movie stars with their names printed in bold characters so that the new Christians could select the name that they liked best for their new lives. The village was now teeming with celebrity names–Gregory Peck and Henry Fonda could be found selling fruit in the market, and Lana Turner worked as a waitress at the Restaurante El Rio Azul. The heroes of the past–the apostles, martyrs and saints–languished in the corners of the abandoned church, like dolls in an antique shop.

I never knew which Elisabeth my Maria modeled herself after. In place of her native dress she wore skirts and blouses which she bought from an Iranian peddler. She also started wearing make-up, which contrasted with her beautiful dark skin to the degree that she seemed to be wearing a mask. She happily dedicated herself fully to the care of Rolando, still leaving at night, however, out of fear of the noises in my house. Just as well, because Margarita had moved in.

I had sought permission to visit La China. I had gone to Solola and spent hours sitting on the wooden benches outside the Comisaria waiting for the Comisario General to sign the slip of paper allowing a short visit. A tremulous flood of indigent relatives of drunks and petty thieves shared with me the worn-out benches in a fraternity of resignation.

"Y usted a quien va'a ver?"

"Un mi sobrino."

"Que hizo?"

"Se entro a una casa, y se robo unas cosas."

"Que desgracia!"

"Pues si, pero que se le va a hacer."

"Y usted?"

"Es un hecho de sangre."

They would tell me the small offenses their relatives had committed, breaking and entering, stealing, getting drunk and disorderly. But when one dared ask the offense of my friend and I answered "a deal of blood"–*un hecho de sangre*–they gathered themselves up and gave me extra room on the bench.

El Comisario finally returned from wherever he had gone, and one by one we paraded in his presence to plead our requests.

La Carcel Santa Teresita sat across the lake in between two volcanoes. As women's prisons go, it wasn't as bad as others I had seen. Four pretty white houses with red tile roofs were surrounded by tiny gardens of lettuce, radishes, spring onions, beets and spinach, proving that all which grew in freedom could grow here also. The women, dressed in their own tribal clothing, looked like captive birds as they busied themselves working at the same trades they had pursued in their villages. Some, sitting like lizards, with half their body erect, wove on back strap looms; others shaped clay into pottery, and still others–the bakers and cooks–attended ovens like beehives that spewed pale blue smoke with the aroma of distant homes.

Four guards in dark green uniforms with high black boots stood like pillars at the four points of the courtyard and were soon forgotten while older women dressed also in dark green directed the activities.

La China had cut her hair short with bangs in the front like a page.

"What a place to meet..." she said.

"You look well, do you suffer much here?" I asked.

"The lack of freedom, that is all. It is not as if I had been free at El Farolito; at least here I sleep well. But freedom is like a drug, like heroin or opium–people will sacrifice anything for it."

She remained silent for a while; she never looked prettier, maybe because now she had joined defeated humanity.

"You will look after Rolando, won't you?"

I remembered when I promised to teach her to read. It was the same now.

"I may send him to live away. *Vale*?" I used the word *vale*, a Spanish word that is binding.

"Whatever you say."

"Where will you send him?" she asked.

"America."

"Is America a good land for children?"

"Some parts of America are like fairyland for children to grow in; others are a horrible hell."

"Our land is good for children; even I cannot complain."

She shrugged her shoulders and a strap of her blouse broke loose. Clothes didn't stay naturally on her, as if her body were in constant rebellion.

"I was happy as a child at the household where my mother left me. As I grew up, the boys in the house and their friends started to learn how to be men with me. I was proud to teach them, even as I myself was learning about being a woman.

"Our land is good to children," she repeated, "but childhood doesn't last long here. I know you will send Rolando to the part of America that is good to children. My heart is at ease."

"Would you like to see him?"

"Maybe once more. It should be soon... I won't be here much longer."

"Are they sending you somewhere else?"

"No, it is not them." She glanced around, and then added: "I must keep my secrets even from you...for your own good."

We kissed farewell; it was as if she had changed, and kissing her was now permitted. Her lips were salty and bitter like those of someone who had cried, but La China, to my knowledge, never cried for long.

XII

XOCOMYL

El Termometro Feliz was a thirty-two foot motor sailor, altered by Uno who could never let well enough alone when it came to engines. It had been a fine motor launch when he first got his hands on it, but he rigged it as a sloop, and, in lieu of a keel, he built a heavy center-board which could be lowered when needed to make the boat stable under sail. He had called her *El Termometro Feliz*, which, translated into English, meant the "Happy Thermometer," a name that puzzled me to no end and was never explained by Uno.

He had lent it to me, and little by little, as women and boats have a way of doing, it moved into my heart, and I ended up feeling that it was my own. It was fortunate that I had her. The guerrillas had blown the bridge on the road to Santa Teresita, and now the prison was accessible only by water.

I had sailed across the lake for my visit with La China, and I sailed back, barely holding to the light breeze blowing east. I needed the time and the tranquil freedom sailing gives those born under a wind sign, and so, willfully ignoring the engine, I set sail across the lake hoping for the *Xocomyl*, that strange wind that comes from nowhere and builds the calm lake into a stormy sea, covered with white caps and foam, as if the volcanoes had spat on the waters.

The *Tzutuhil* called it "Mad Wind."

I didn't reckon it was to be more than a light sail, but when the *Xocomyl* rose, my inner self sprang to life, and, as I trimmed sails and steered the tiller beating to a reckless weather, voices within me came to life, revealing secrets I had hidden from myself.

I had not wished to know the hopes I had built for La China and me, but now, when sailing alone, I realized she would no longer wait in the early sun of happy mornings for me to spin my tales of distant lands and adventure. Anguish built in me as if the weather had gotten inside my chest. The Mad Wind raked the lake waters into a frenzy of spray, and, howling like the screams of an angry little ocean, the water splashing in my face was sweet. It is easier for a man to cry when sailing in a true sea; one cannot taste one's tears.

Come away, O human child.

I thought of Mary and Tommy and Rolando, and of the life that could be theirs among the rolling mountains, the Siskiyous, a kind and gentle land of honest people, and my heart, like La China had said, was at ease.

Of all men, I believe those who live on the ocean understand life better than any other, and that even when they seek the safety of land, their hearts cry for the intense struggle of the dark waters offshore. They know, that in life or at sea, there is no final triumph or defeat.

This is not true of those who live by a lake. It is very tragic to be a lake captive, forever among mountains. There is a sense of hopelessness, a quiet despair that reaches out from the gray waters like a phantom, to weaken the spirit of the men who live in the villages onshore. The lake is not part of their lives.

They fear drowning, or even worse, they fear *Cauok, el dueño del lago*, the powerful spirit who owns the lake, who has the power to steal their souls.

The men would watch with anguish as Margarita or I sailed our boat defying *Xocomyl*, and when we reached shore they avoided us, lest *Cauok's* anger might also reach our friends.

I reached shore and, as I tidied my boat, the wind departed, and once again the lake set itself to rest in indifference.

I never doubted Margarita was capable of affirming herself if she chose to. She seldom did. It seemed she regarded life as an incident rather than a finality, and yet, she would take stands on matters that most others took lightly. Elisabeth's change of name and her new dress and her painting herself as a clown offended Margarita's sense of fairness, and she resented the moral intrusion of the missionaries with the same intensity that she did the destruction of forests or the brutal rape of the land.

But, I am getting ahead of my narrative.

I reached my house at sunset, which says nothing about time near the lake. The sun takes forever to set there. One would say it stops at every home to bid good night, kissing the land on both cheeks as Spaniards do– and Frenchmen and Russians–and then watching as the land blushes and retires to dream until another day.

The red gate was open. In the middle of my garden, the camper rubbed elbows with an old pine tree and a rose bush. I knew Tommy and Mary had arrived, and my heart beat with joy. Mary was in the kitchen teaching Elisabeth how to apply make-up. She herself wore none. Yet with the peculiar understanding that exists among women, she perceived the need of the young *Tzutuhil* maiden to change into something she was not. Elisabeth was heading into a *Xocomyl* more confusing than any Mad Wind she ever knew.

Margarita guessed I was back and rushed from somewhere to embrace me with tenderness. Ever since her return from the clinic in Temple, she had opened to me without apprehension.

I heard the welcome noises of men. Upstairs in my room Uno, Alizarin and Tommy were rolling dice and gambling insignificant amounts with the intensity I had seen among players at Biarritz. Rolando, meanwhile, slept in his rabbit box, biding his time.

I guess home is more than a place where they have to take you in.

Short of a miracle, as Jesus performed when he fed the multitude with two fish and five loaves of bread, there is nothing better to feed unexpected guests on short notice than a Spanish *tortilla de patatas*.

I left my friends engrossed in their dice game and went to the kitchen, escorted by my lovely acolytes. Elisabeth had gone at the first sign of darkness. Margarita and Mary poured themselves a glass of wine and sat at the kitchen table to sip and chat and keep me company while I cooked. I chanted the recipe I had learned from Nena, my old friend from Castilla la Vieja.

"One medium onion for two large potatoes and five eggs. Slice them finely and simmer in olive oil!"

Mary and Margarita were not listening, so I kept the rest to myself and became so immersed in my cooking that I didn't hear what they talked about. Once in a while their laughter, alive like gypsy music, held my attention. I smiled without knowing why.

In a large bowl I beat the five eggs. When the onions and potatoes started to brown, I poured them into the eggs and mixed them evenly. This I poured into a pan hot with olive oil. As the tortilla started to set, I seasoned it with salt and pepper. The trick was now to wait and guess when the tortilla was done on one side. Then, using a dish to cover the pan, I turned my tortilla over and slid it back for the other side to brown.

I made three, in no time, fifteen eggs and three onions and six potatoes!

Elizabeth decided to throw a party to celebrate Rolando's birthday–without regard for the true date–which was in August.

She took care of the arrangements. The table where the gifts were displayed looked as if Tom Sawyer had emptied the pockets of his trousers to show his treasures. Every child had brought a present, and Elisabeth arranged them on the kitchen table. It had been her idea to have a *piñata* for Rolando, and she had invited the children of the neighborhood who arrived at four on Sunday afternoon, escorted by their parents. I didn't recognize them with their washed faces and no dogs, yet their presents were a happy ensemble of the bits and ends of their lives: a bit of pretty red string, a small ball of black beeswax, a shiny river stone, five yellow candies wrapped in a blue paper, a live lizard inside a bottle, a red bird's feather, a small piece of leather, and two small candles. I was reminded of the offerings at the church's atrium on the harvest ceremony.

The *piñata* was a turkey made of painted cardboard, its innards a clay pot filled with wrapped candy and confetti. It was hanging from a rope strung between two trees. A line tied in the middle, when pulled, jerked the bird out of harm's way, not that he was in danger. The blindfolded children, after being spun around a couple of times, swung the broomstick in every direction but the one where the turkey hung.

"What makes turkeys such natural victims?" Mary asked. "I wonder," she mused, "what sort of country would America be now if we had a gentle and accommodating turkey as our national symbol, as Ben Franklin wanted, instead of the predatory eagle."

I didn't know the answer.

"At least we would not have an endangered species as a national symbol," I said.

"Thanksgiving could be Revival Day," she said. "We could eat our hero yearly and start anew, purified!"

Our musings could have gone on forever. but Pedrito, the child who delivered the fish, whacked the *piñata* open, and a rain of candy and confetti fell on the delighted children who greedily threw themselves to the grass grabbing, holding, scooping and chewing.

Now came the time when the mothers, embarrassed by the passions of their children, helped pour *agua de canela* -- a sweet cinnamon water -- and served frail *barquillos*, sugar cones wrapped in the shape of long fingers. The fathers, who regarded the whole performance as alien and below their dignity, drank *aguitas*, multicolored soft drinks spiked on the sneak.

Elizabeth was in seventh heaven at the success of her party. I wished she still were Maria the *Tzutuhil*. But all considerations aside, a Sunday afternoon without a bull fight, no matter what, can be longer than a night without bread.

And now...those of you readers who have followed all this living with me, I must remind you that I don't make life. Someone who is very cruel does–hard as it may be to understand–but who can understand the sudden bite of a viper?

I had gone away with Tommy and Mary to the Capital City to stand in line and pay tribute to bureaucracy in order to get a passport for Rolando, who couldn't read or write and was only learning to talk. The country had to protect its children from flying away; it was bad enough that they died at home!

The city was no longer the same place of my childhood. She had grown deformed like an adolescent dwarf, with arms and legs in disproportion, stretching in *barrios* and *asentamientos*–the slums where the peasants had been lured with false promises by politicians.

My childhood city had deserved a better fate. It had been virtuous and kind, a gentle town of *araucarias* and trees that bloomed blue in the fall. It had been a town of church bells tolling at dawn to accompany the prayers of old women for the eternal rest of Souls in Purgatory, and evenings resounding with their hurried feminine steps as they returned home from the chapels to prepare dinner: soups and meats and bread, sprinkled with kind thoughts for those who had nothing to eat.

Bureaucracy is the same the world over. Its buildings are pale and neglected with faded paint like the parched faces of its clerks and secretaries. Papers are signed in triplicate at one window and payment is made in another. A triplicate receipt is then exchanged for a pink coupon at yet another window, where a crone, posing as an indifferent clerk, instructs one to return in two days.

I wanted to show my friends the sites I loved as a child, but I could no longer find them. Perhaps they hid from me so I couldn't see how they had aged, as old friends do, or perhaps they had died. The cathedral was still there, her towers again destroyed. They had been rebuilt many times, but as soon as they were completed, temblors again toppled them.

Perhaps Pipo had something to do with it. He was a dwarf, the sacristan who rang the bells at the cathedral. My friends and I were healthy children, students at a school next to the church, *El Colegio de Infantes.*

"Peepoh, Pipo, who made you so ugly?"

"Was it the devil, Pipo?"

We chanted and danced around the tormented dwarf. In despair, he would run to his refuge, high in his towers, and ring his bells, louder and louder, to drown our song and laughter. One day one of the revolving bells caught him in the back as he tolled in anguish, and he fell among us like a broken doll.

I drove my friends to Antigua, the colonial city escorted by two volcanoes, where time ended and never started again, and where one day is the same as another and all are full of grace like an *Ave Maria.* I told them about *El Hermano* Pedro, the third order Franciscan who protected the Indians during colonial times, and I showed them his grave where the *Quiche* still come to complain and ask for his help, knocking at the tombstone as if to a door.

It was in Antigua, at a small goldsmith shop, that Mary asked: "Quince, shouldn't you buy a ring for Margarita?"

Mary always asked when she meant one should do it.

"I already gave her one," I answered. I had given her my ring, my grandfather's, a gold ring with the family crest.

"I saw it. It is a lovely ring, and she loves it, but one of these days her finger will fall off–it must weigh half a pound!"

I had to admit it was heavy. I had seldom worn it myself. Yet the night we accepted our love I had nothing more to give, and she had received it as a sign of my good faith.

We stopped by a jeweler in town and chose a simple gold band. The goldsmith inscribed my name on the inside. After all, I didn't wish for Margarita to lose a finger on my account.

The new city at night was loud and frantic like a disco. Our hotel offered no protection from the noise. After two nights we drove away, almost in fear, back to the country, to a life we could understand.

There was no smoke coming from my house's chimney as we took the last bend in the mountain and started our descent to the village.

"I wonder where Margarita is," I asked of no one.

"*Tranquilo!*" said Mary, "She will never be far from you."

But, somehow, my heart wondered. As we entered the village, a soldier signaled us to stop and follow him. *El Capitan* Lobo sat at a small table in a terribly vacant room of white walls and emptiness. A fan whirled from the ceiling.

"Quince," he said, slowly and gently, "I have very bad news....We have lost a friend."

I can accept pain as well as any other man, but I don't know how to paint horror. Goya the Spaniard did, as no one had before him, and he went mad. I have forgotten much of what Lobo said; I heard his voice resounding like an echo. Perhaps like Goya, I also went mad.

Margarita had died. And Rolando. Lobo spoke, his voice breaking, tired of being a soldier. Margarita had sailed with Rolando to Santa Teresita, the jail across the lake between the volcanoes, where La China had waited for them for a last visit with her child.

"I signed the permission for their visit," Lobo said.

"*La guerrilla* attacked the prison by surprise and shelled the lake to stop reinforcements from reaching the garrison by water. You know last week they blew the bridge on the road. We can reach Santa Teresita only by water now.

"They know much about war tactics; they have been at it for a long time.

"They fired blindly. They seemed thrilled by the shrapnel rippling the waters." Lobo looked at me with sadness.

"When we returned the fire, they were not so happy. Our batteries reach farther. *El Termometro Feliz* was caught in the crossfire. A shell ignited her. There was an explosion–smoke and blindness. And, when that cleared, there was nothing. In the turmoil at the prison, the guerrillas escaped. La China went with them. She gave herself in gratitude for her freedom. She didn't know she had already paid.

"I do not know who killed Margarita...and the child. Whether it was them or us, their bullets or ours. In this war only the innocent die. Not one of our soldiers died...not one of the guerrillas."

Lobo stretched his hand and posed it in mine. I felt his sweat on my skin and was repulsed.

"I want your forgiveness, Quince."

He spoke softly. But even as he pleaded, holding my hand in his, officers and sergeants walked in. First one, and then, two. Lobo released my hand and gave them sealed envelopes with new battle orders.

Rage invaded me for the hypocrisy of his shallow repentance. Like a lion's roar, I heard the voice of Yahweh talking to the Prophet Hosea: *This is why I have torn them to pieces by the prophets, why I slaughtered them with the words from my mouth.*

I got up from my chair, heaving myself with one hand on the table. Then I felt the hand of Mary on my wrist.

The Mad Wind wrapped my soul. In my delirium, Yahweh spoke to me through Hosea and promised to break their altars down and destroy their sacred stones. I saw the heart of the land as a divided heart. I heard the words of their *presidentes* and guerrilla commandants, and they spoke the same false words. And I heard the voices of the Indians asking, *What can you do for us?*

"I will write a book and be a good neighbor and create a Great Alliance!"

"Words, words! False oaths! Alliances! And judgments! Like poisonous weeds that thrive in the furrows of the field."

Then Hosea, the Prophet, was silent. Slowly, guided by the voice of Mary, and strengthened by the presence of Uno, I staggered once more into life, with clowns and firecrackers and colors blue and yellow, into the world of fairies.

One morning I went to the market. "Jesus loves you...," the strangled voice of the parrot repeated. "Jonah, row the boat ashore... Jonah, row–hallelujah!"

I recognized the two men, the old man and the young one. The old man was talking to a small group of ragged villagers.

"They were going to *fusilarla*. But then, as a last grace, she asked the captain of the firing squad for a piece of charcoal. She drew a little sailboat on the white wall of her cell, got in it and sailed away through the window bars."

The listeners nodded their heads knowingly. Then they laughed and busied themselves with their chores. La China was now a legend. The older man got up with difficulty. He staggered toward me, reaching for walls and the irons of windows.

"El hombre que ama las iguanas." He pointed at me. "The man who loves the iguanas!" he repeated, and laughed convulsively.

He almost fell. But he held on to my shoulder and embraced me. "If you can love iguanas, you also can love us." I raised my hand to wipe the fetid infamy of his spit from my face and pushed him away. He fell to the ground. He looked hurt and humiliated as he crawled back to his parrot. He picked up a rock and threw it at me.

The blood from my brow mixed with the dust of the village.

A heavy military truck drove toward the lake.

PART TWO:

TEN BACKYARD STORIES FROM PANIMACHE

I

SIGUANAWA, THE SPIRIT TEMPTRESS

The night was sultry, feminine and tender, like a mulatto woman from Camaguey. The air was perfumed by the white cornucopia flowers of the "sleep tree," and an early moon gave only enough light for me to walk, guessing at shadows and dangers.

I was on my way to supper at *el comedor* de Don Julio. I liked his cooking, and his eatery was not far from my house, which was good. The land was tormented by a sordid war between the soldiers of the government and those of the guerrillas, and the pretty village, caught in the middle of the conflict, suffered from frights and rumors. Night walking was risky; the town was said to be crawling with all sorts of unsavory characters, and to make matters worse, a man had drowned the previous night in the lake, and his shadow–as everybody knew–had to wander in confusion and pain for nine days before going to its eternal rest. I walked, stepping loudly on the cobblestones so as not to startle with a sudden appearance those who, like me, also walked in the semi-darkness, fearing an encounter with the ghost of the drowned man.

The village in Guatemala with the strange name "Panimache," her innocence defiled by merchants, soldiers and missionaries, rested by the lake with the perverse neglect of a young lover lying by an old man. Don Julio, the owner and cook of the restaurant, treated me as family. He was a robust man who enjoyed savoring his own cooking more than selling it. He was one-fourth Indian. It showed in his temperament, black hair and intense eyes. His lips often smiled under a droopy mustache that gave him the appearance of a benign Pancho Villa. He was no longer young but disclaimed aging.

Lucia set my table under the arbor. She was an orphan, an Indian child who had come to live at Don Julio's household after her own home was devastated by the war. Although she was eleven or twelve years old, she seemed younger because she was small and had the figure of a child, with large black eyes and long black hair kept tidily braided. She seldom smiled, but when she did, you saw her very white teeth scattered here and there, as if someone had thrown a handful of them into her mouth with the same abandon with which she threw maize for the chickens. It was nice to see her, safe and blossoming now, dressed in her colorful blue skirt and embroidered red blouse, moving with the rapid grace of a squirrel among the pots and pans.

Some time before, a visiting lady from Switzerland had been very moved when she saw Lucia working, and commented that the children in her native Basilea at Lucia's age could hardly tie their shoes. In her effusion she tried to press some money into Lucia's hand.

"For you, dear child, for you to keep," she had said. Lucia recoiled as if touched by a tarantula, and when the woman insisted, Lucia bit her hand. The lady cried in pain, "You ugly ape...!"

I had explained to her that Lucia didn't yet know the meaning of money. The lady demanded a disinfectant, but Don Julio only had ointment that he explained was good for coyote bites and nothing more.

Lucia had set my table under the arbor next to the patio where the lemon trees grew, and the orange trees, and crotons with dotted leaves, and giant leaves that looked as trees but were only those that had grown around trees and stolen their sap, becoming as tall as trees but lacking their nobility. It's the nature of vines to be devious and cruel; they hurt the trees that they embrace, and yet they bring to the land the vitality of the tropics–the primeval aroma of new rain, visions of hidden temples and forgotten rites, jaguars and strange birds, and of paintings by Rousseau.

There were three more little tables scattered among the trees. They were pleasant to sit at when the weather was warm and the breeze blew from the lake, painted Moorish blue and offering a vivid contrast to the ochre dirt packed under them as hard as tiles.

A man sat at one of them. He wore blue serge trousers and a blue coat. His shirt was white and buttoned up, yet he wore no tie. There was a stain where the tie should have been–a fresh stain where he had spilled the coffee he had drunk in an effort to sober up. He was still very drunk and found it difficult to sit straight on the hard wooden chair. With his elbows on the table, he held with both hands a half-empty bottle of beer. At frequent intervals he looked over his shoulder and shivered. One could easily take him for a fugitive, an image frequently seen in those unsettled days. But I had met him in Solola where he kept his shop, El Ultimo Recuerdo, and I knew he was an established carpenter, a coffin maker. Don Julio went over to him.

With an effort, the carpenter got up, and the men embraced fraternally.

"Courage, *amigo*," Don Julio said.

The man held to him. He tried to steady himself but found it impossible and slumped back in his chair with a resigned shrug.

"*Estoy muy borracho*," he explained. "Very, very drunk," he insisted, to leave no doubt about his condition. "But I'm also very grateful to you, my old friend...." He didn't explain the reason for his gratitude, looking bewildered, like an actor who had forgotten his lines.

Don Julio seemed vaguely disappointed. "You would have done the same for me...," he said, unsure of what his friend's gratitude was about. "You must have courage, *amigo*," Don Julio repeated, patting him on the back without much conviction. The man shook his head slowly to express his doubt that he had what it took.

"So, you left the wake?" Don Julio asked gently.

"They can have the whole *velorio* to themselves," the man answered. "I am the father of the deceased, and I am paying for the whole wake, but to see the way they carried on, you would have thought I wasn't even related." He shook his head to accentuate his disappointment.

"It's because of the times," Don Julio agreed. "It's not as it used to be."

"They don't seem to have any sentiment," affirmed Don Moises. "You may say it's the times. They call it progress not to have sentiments! Not like we were. Maybe it's because they have lost respect for the old ways."

"They don't believe in God or honor," Don Julio said.

"They don't believe in respect for their elders," added Don Moises.

"It's a sad generation. One wonders what will become of them," Don Julio concluded.

Don Moises tried to think what else to object to; he raised his hand twice, but nothing came to mind. "Ah...I am very grateful to you, dear friend, and to your distinguished wife, for the wreath you sent."

"Think nothing of it," Don Julio said modestly. "You would have done the same in my place."

"I pray you are never in my sad situation." Don Moises searched his pockets until he found a red bandanna. He blew his nose and dried his eyes. "*Que se le va a hacer*," he said. "There's nothing one can do now but pray for the eternal rest of my poor Luciano."

"How did he drown?" Don Julio asked softly.

"The whole truth will never been known."

Don Julio looked around suspiciously and then asked, "Was there a mystery?"

"The explanation they gave doesn't make sense," said Don Moises.

"What did they say?"

"They made him appear very ignorant and dumb."

"He never was too smart," said Don Julio cautiously.

"If one is to tell the truth, no, he never was too smart," Don Moises agreed. "He was handsome, though." Then he added, "The way they said it, he drowned due to ignorance and pride. I have my doubts, though..." He let his words trail.

"And how was that?" Don Julio asked.

"Alcohol also played a role."

"Had he been drinking?"

"That's what they said." Don Moises was reticent. "It was already late in the evening when he and his friend Calixto Gomar–the one they call Chicho–went to the lake for a walk."

Don Moises moved restlessly in his chair, then asked shyly, "With your permission, could I have another *aguita?*" He pronounced it "Ah-we-tah," which meant "tiny water."

Don Julio clapped his hands, and Sofia appeared as if she had sprung out of the hard soil. She brought a bottle of beer, Cerveza Cabro, in a green bottle with a laughing goat on the label.

"Where was I?" Don Moises asked rhetorically. "Yes, they had been drinking, but according to Chicho, who told the story, they still had their wits together. They walked around the lake all the way to the docks. They heard music coming from the new Hotel del Lago, and when they were closer, they could see a party going on in the illuminated dining room. Chicho said it was a great party, a *gringo* party, with lovely women with blonde hair, tall and slim, dancing, lightheartedly, showing their legs through the slits in their short skirts." Don Moises searched his pockets for his bandanna but couldn't find it. "What do you suppose makes them so pretty?" he asked.

"They say it's the food they eat," Don Julio said. "Hard to believe, but that's what they say."

"Maybe they say that just to hook us into buying food. I, for one, wouldn't put it past them," Don Moises said.

"Well," he continued, "one of the women came out to the terrace to get fresh air, and she came very close to where Chicho and my son Luciano stood in the dark before she noticed them. She came so close they could smell her perfume and look at her blue eyes. She was dressed in gold lamé, and her skirt was small as a handkerchief. Her legs were tanned and bare, and she wore high heels.

"'*Hola, muchachos!*' she said in hesitant Spanish. '*Como estas tu, muchacho?*' she asked my son. '*Estas muy guapo, muchacho.*' Then, shifting to English, 'You are really handsome. Would you like to dance?'

"Luciano, my defunct son, didn't know English," Don Moises affirmed.

"'No speak,' he said.

"'*Quiero tu bailar?*' She took his hand, wrapped her arm around him, and led him in two dancing steps. A man came out from the dining room.

"'For goodness' sakes, Diana, what in the devil do you think you're doing?'

"'*Tengo que ir, pero regresar...regreso?*' Her Spanish was as bad as my son's English, but he understood she had promised to return.

"'Do you think she will come back?' Luciano asked Chicho. He was sure she would return if only he waited long enough. They reached the end of the beach. Chicho wanted to go home, but Luciano wished to stay and wait. Chicho left. He didn't want to tell Luciano that the dancing woman would never come.

"She was like *La Siguanawa*, a ghost that appears to men in the guise of a seductive woman and leads them to their deaths," Don Moises explained.

"Chicho thought of the woman far in the mountains in the jungle who was a commandant of the guerillas. She also was called *La Siguanawa,* because she had taken many young men from the village with promises of freedom and lands. But, like the ghost, she brought only death and abandonment." Don Moises paused. "Chicho was afraid of his thoughts," he concluded.

Don Moises again searched himself for his bandanna, found it and stretched it on the table. It looked like the bloodied map of the land.

"This is what Chicho said happened that night."

"Do you believe it?" Don Julio asked, raising his eyebrows.

"I don't know what to believe any more," Don Moises answered, lowering his voice. "Luciano, my poor son, had been talking about joining the guerrillas in the jungle. Perhaps someone overheard him. Perhaps even his own friend Chicho... Whom can you trust these days?"

"Then you think he might...that they might have drowned him?"

"I don't like my thoughts." Don Moises seemed all at once sober and dignified. "I must go back now to the *velorio*. They may start wondering where I am and get suspicious. Next thing you know, I also will be floating in the lake or in a river, and people will say I drowned because I was stupid."

Don Julio came to my table and sat down on the empty chair. He spoke in a deliberately soft voice.

"Did you hear what we talked about?" he asked me.

"Was it a secret? Of course, I did."

"I wish you hadn't. I must have spoiled your dinner."

"It didn't."

"What do you think?"

I didn't know what to answer.

Don Julio looked around with concern.

"I think," he said, "I think *La Siguanawa* got him."

"Do you mean the commandant of the guerrillas?"

"No, I don't mean her."

"The government people? Is Chicho an informer?"

"How would I know?" Don Julio shifted uneasily on his chair. "What I mean is that after everything has been said and told, it's wiser to believe *La Siguanawa*, the ghost, got him."

II

THE EMPTY CAGE

Mornings are not bad. They begin early, sometime between three and three-thirty, with darkness still there, before the birds start to sing. They start with noises that are good: the soft calls of cows to calves, the dragging of wooden milking stools over cobblestones, and the melody of milk squirting on the tin pails. Somewhere in the dark yard, horses change their stance with the sound of iron hitting rock. It's good in the mornings, but the whole day lies ahead, and by ten, one knows what's coming.

You don't know what hot is until you have been in Mazatenango at three in the afternoon. You try to breathe air, but all you get is steam, and, as you gasp, you could swear a witch is roasting you in a bed of red-hot coals.

Mazatenango is in the southern part of Guatemala, the very belly button of the tropics. The name means "Land of Deer," but don't expect to see deer flying through the air, because Mazatenango is jungle country, and the deer, as well as snakes and jaguars and all free animals, have many places to hide from peering eyes. Mazatenango also hides, and very few know where it is, but sometimes hiding is not enough.

Now, it happened that one summer day, the tyrant president of the land ordered that every municipality of the country should build, at the entrance of its most important town, a monument to symbolize what was characteristic of the place. The order was haltingly read in every corner of the towns by a corporal with an escort of four soldiers. One blew a bugle, another played upon his drum, while the other two presented arms. And so, with fearful shivers, each 'presidente municipal' taxed the town residents into despair in order to build their department's symbol.

Solola, to the north, built a statue of two Indians, one playing a drum and the other a flute. Quetzaltenango, in the highlands, cast a beautiful image of an Indian woman in full tribal regalia. In Mazatenango, the presidente municipal and the Honorable Council of Citizens naturally decided the symbol should be a deer.

Bronze doesn't come cheap, and Mazatecs do not like to waste their money. The town had fallen into hard times with a drop in coffee prices, and since the United Fruit Co. had left, the price of bananas was also *por los suelos*; literally, "gone to ground level." After many siestas and meetings, the Señores oficiales were not getting anywhere. The treasury had no will or money to cast a statue of a deer, and the town residents, bled by malaria and heat, were immune to threats from authorities.

The apathy that tropical sun can bring to weigh on the shoulders of men is like a cross of indifference carried by everyone, yet it creates a certain indolent courage. And so, even in the face of possible presidential rage, the principals of the town met twice weekly at El Buen Gustito, the town's ice cream parlor, and yawned and frowned, discussing the merits of this or that solution to the problem of the statue and did nothing, absolutely nothing.

The gatherings, however, became the talk of the town. An accordion player showed up one night, bellowing tangos. Soon after, the pretty young women of the pueblo, their tiny, sultry figures riding on nervous tendons of desire and apprehension, appeared at El Buen Gustito–tropical nymphets with a taste for ice cream–inevitably followed by young men with washed olive faces and starched shirts.

No man, given a chance, can resist the orator in himself when in front of an audience of adoring young females. The aging members of the congregation of Señores oficiales were no exception, yet even the most inspired could find little poetry in arguing the costs of the bronze statue of a deer, until one night when the laureate poet Don Gerundio Albergue was invited to join the advisory group as an artistic consultant.

Don Gerundio was tall, slender and bent, like a sugar cane at harvest time. He was the only poet in Mazatenango and thus had been laureate year after year on Independence Day, when he read his "Oda a la Libertad Lograda." On those special occasions he wore his tinsel crown of laurel with the same pride Don Quijote had worn a barber's dish as a helmet. Yet, in spite of the tragic error of his deportment, Don Gerundio inspired a climate of kindness and innocence, because his soul was not of this world.

That evening when Don Gerundio made his speech was especially hot, and he must have suffered, dressed in a black jacket and wearing a poet's ribbon tie on a white starched shirt. That night he also wore his laurel crown.

"Oh, gentle daughters of Mnemosyne and Zeus," he exclaimed, opening his arms like the wings of a grouse. "Oh gentle Muses of the arts and poetry! Hear my prayer for inspiration and guidance!"

He must have prayed from his heart, because soon inspiration reached him.

"We shall not have bronze. We shall not have wood, or any metal," he declaimed in his beautiful, sonorous voice. "Not even gold could represent our essence, for we do not believe in material survival, but in the powers of the spirit. We shall have a living symbol of our land–blood and nerves and agility and..." Here his inspiration faltered. Lowering his timbre, in a confidential tone, he added, "And it will be very economical."

His inspired solution was to have, instead of a statue, a cage with a live deer–a cage in the form of a triangle, but without a roof–to signify "a pyramid of wisdom opened to the skies of eternity."

The day of the inauguration arrived, as everything does in this life, sooner or later. It arrived with bands and ribbons; it arrived with hopes and pride. It arrived with heat and disillusion. At the first explosion of firecrackers, the deer jumped out of its cage and into the jungle, like a lost dream.

Nights are not so bad in Mazatenango. There are flowers that open only at this time, and their fragrance runs unopposed. Nights start when the heat is over, sometimes as late as seven. The cicadas call each other, and a breeze touches the leaves of tropical trees. On Tuesdays and Thursdays there is a band concert in the plaza, and the young people play among trees of jasmine. Late every evening there is a Rosary being said at the church in the center of town, and women pray for the rest of souls in purgatory.

Men are very alone in the early night. They walk back and forth on the red Spanish tiles in the corridors of their homes, not hungry or thirsty, but waiting to be. Waiting for something–perhaps a day without heat.

Mazatenango has known better times. One can tell, because all of its streets are cobbled, and now the stones roll loose like bad teeth. The town is indifferent to its past and holds no hope for the future. It asks only to be left alone, to be left behind in the heat and dust, a tired town, empty of dreams. But one cannot leave her. One loves the pueblo as one loves an old wife.

The empty cage is still standing at the entrance of the town. It will always be there.

III

LOT'S WIFE

There are sad days in the village, mostly in November, when the lake wraps itself in gray clouds and fog rolls down the streets like a soul in pain, and one hears plaintive tolling of church bells and wonders who of the neighbors in Panimache has said his last farewells.

Faces and names appear fleetingly in one's mind. No, not Perico the telegraphist–too young, still. Anselmo, the barman? Seemed very healthy two nights ago. Jacinta la Araucaria, owner of El Farolito? She will never die. Gustavo, the pharmacist? Not him, but perhaps his wife, Gumercinda; she was coughing badly. Probably a cold. Then, with a shrug of the shoulders, *quien sabe*? At least this time it's not me.

On one such day I walked the cobbled street known as Calle del Farolito, enjoying the heavy fog, which felt good inside the lungs and was kind to the eyes. I wore my Basque beret, which kept my ears warm, and the heavy wool jacket that my Irish friend Robbie had given me as a gift when we went trout fishing in his homeland. My trousers were formless in the comfort of their amplitude, warm and wrinkled.

In the empty Calle de los Perdidos, incongruous, like sudden laughter, a wooden sign bearing the image of a red rooster playing a yellow guitar announced El Gallo Contento, the eatery owned by Don Julio

Hernandez Zapoj. He was half Indian, half something else; a large man with sad eyes and a droopy mustache–noble, like an ox–true to his heart even when it went wrong, a philosopher when given the chance, and a stupendous cook.

He waited for me at the entrance of the patio, where in better weather little tables were scattered among exotic plants and tall trees.

"*Bienvenido*, Señor Quince!" He greeted me in his deep voice, as if he hadn't seen me in years. I was a regular customer, but he displayed the same gracious enthusiasm every time he saw me. "Please come inside, before you catch *pulmonia*."

Pulmonia was the favorite illness in Panimache. Even though it meant pneumonia, I had seen cases of appendicitis, gunshot wounds, and even suicides diagnosed as *pulmonia*.

"This is a weather made for *pulmonia*, like poor Señor Lot–may his soul rest in peace–had a chance to learn."

So it had been Lot for whom the bell had tolled. I had known Lotario before he shortened his name to Lot.

Don Julio set my table in a small room adjacent to the kitchen. It was a pleasant little place, with white walls dominated by a reproduction of Pietro Giacomo's *Destruccion de Sodoma y Gomorra,* a dramatic painting of the fiery destruction of the sinful cities. In the foreground a bearded prophet with a satisfied look raised one hand to heaven. Lot, a young man, covered his eyes in terror. At some distance, the salt statue of a nude woman, Lot's wife, stretched her arms toward the destroyed cities. She was beautifully formed, sensuous even in her desperate farewell to the cities she had loved, with streets now twisted like burning serpents and lovely fountains run dry.

Whom did she leave behind? I asked myself. A friend, a lover? Why did she turn? Did she wish to share their fate? Or did she mean to escape from prophets and vindictive gods? It was better that she died. For a free woman from Sodoma, life among the righteous would have been hell.

Don Julio brought me a bottle, which I examined with interest. It was genuine wine from Munera, in Navarra, close to the Pyrenees. He decanted it, serving the ruby vintage in a tall stemmed glass. Respectfully, he withdrew two steps, observing me with an expectant gaze while I tasted the full-bodied wine, rich and warm to the heart.

"Thank you, Don Julio," I said, moved by his thoughtfulness. "This is a great gesture of yours." He knew my family was from Navarra.

"I am proud to serve this wine to you," he said and left me to attend to his kitchen. My thoughts promptly flew to Lot.

Lotario's father, Don Baldomero Renduela, was the public notary in Panimache. A portly Galician, thick of accent, honest, Catholic and convinced of the Pope's infallibility, he had settled in the village as its only notary. After his German first wife died of a fall from a horse Don Baldomero, left to raise young Lotario by himself, had married Gerlinde, his wife's second sister, who died two months after the wedding from choking on a chicken bone.

Once more Don Baldomero had tried fortune, with the youngest of the sisters, a scrofulous woman who had reached her twentieth birthday mid respiratory catarrhs and swollen glands. In spite of her chlorosis,

Gineviere Forst de Renduela–Doña Geno, as the villagers promptly rebaptized her–turned out to be very enduring.

Having received a dowry from the three sisters, Don Baldomero, in his late years, was a wealthy man, but this failed to affect his life style or character. He continued to work with the same eagerness of his youth. His office across from the *juzgado civil* was a catacomb of heavy books and registers in the midst of which, perched on a high stool, the notary spent his days and dreamt his nights, entering in a large book the financial transactions of the villagers.

Doña Geno, left to her own resources at home, nursed her catarrhs and instructed her nephew in the manners of the world. Whether because of her European teachings, or perhaps responding to some inherited trait, the only son of the methodical notary developed into a distracted young man, insatiable in his need for feminine affection but without qualities to obtain it, except for those three that Don Ramon del Ville Inclan determined women find irresistible in a man: he was ugly, Catholic, and sentimental.

Life in Panimache is rhythmic and calm. The only disruption is caused by *Xocomyl*, the mad wind that blows from the lake in the afternoons, sometimes bringing rain and other times not, providing guesses and bets among the villagers. In that gentle situation the arrival of *Las Francesas*, a troupe of five lovely French women driving their own cream-colored convertible, license plates 444, was as exciting as a hecatomb!

Soon, the town's white walls looked like posted envelopes, announcing the performances of the feminine troupe. Singing was to be followed by modern dancing and acrobatics, closing with the classical Can Can!

The artists–Ivette, Francine, Melanie, Gabrielle and Coco–had appeared at Le Moulin Rouge in Rue Pigalle, Paris, and also in Rome, Madrid, and the Netherlands *con exito atronador*. The posters were written in Spanish, French and English with the exception of the last phrase, which was untranslatable. This mattered little, because most of the villagers couldn't read and were content with gawking at the pictures of the scantily dressed women. Opening night, however, kept being postponed from night to night and from week to week, until finally it never happened.

It so happened that Mr. Fulton, the Pentecostal minister, accidentally found out the artists' true occupation. During their short stay in the village, he said, they had emptied the pockets of the poor and the rich, broken their hearts, and started an epidemic of sin.

Mr. Fulton was a sad figure of a man. Myopic of eyes, with more head than his body deserved and more belly than head, he was nevertheless a very good orator. On the Sunday following his discovery of the whoring activities of *Las Francesas*, he chose for his sermon "The Destruction of Sodom and Gomorrah." He read from Genesis, Chapter 19, the attempts of the men from Sodoma–young and old–to sodomize the two angels that Yahweh had sent, disguised as young men to scout the condemned cities, and Lot's efforts to protect them. With tears flowing, in a broken voice, Mr. Fulton described how Lot had offered his two virgin daughters to be ravaged instead of his angelic guests, and the refusal of the men from Sodoma to accept the exchange. This attempt to defile his angels had exceeded Yahweh's patience, and the cities were destroyed.

"My dear brothers!" Mr. Fulton concluded. "Let's follow his example and destroy the accursed Sodomites in our midst, for there is sin in ignoring sin, and double sin in pretending blindness, and triple sin and quadruple and infinite sin in ignoring the rage of Yahweh!"

After such intense exhortation he slumped in a chair, exhausted, while his parishioners took to the streets with torches to set fire to the house occupied by *Las Francesas*. Fortunately, the pretty women had been alerted and, neither tardy nor lazy, had packed their assets and taken off in high spirits, driving their cream-colored convertible. Apolonia, their handy woman, followed in a station wagon with their baggage. When they reached the Capital hours later, they discovered with horror that Coco–whom each assumed was in the other vehicle–had been left behind!

Coco was young, frail, blue-eyed and ashen blonde as an archangel in a tableau by Fra Angelico. During her friends' escape, she had been away on an errand of her profession with young Lotario. The two youngsters heard the commotion caused by the wasted rage of the fanatic mob and wisely hid in one of the numerous rooms at Don Baldomero's house.

How long they could have remained undiscovered is only a matter of speculation. The house was immense, and Lotario's quarters in his father's house were fully equipped and comfortable. In it the lovers lived secretly, wrapped in their passion like two worms in a single cocoon.

Free love is exhausting to body and spirit; to survive, love needs sanctions, intrusions, and prohibitions.

A prisoner of secrecy during the day, Coco suffered the contradiction of opposing desires. Her soul rebelled against limits with the agonized fury of a bird that pecks at the wires of its cage, and yet the gentleness in her nature and her sensitive regard for Lotario, whose desperate need for love she perceived, kept her immobile, waiting in silence–waiting, waiting. It was only at night when all was silent that Coco, in rare moments of freedom, wandered in the gardens of the inner yard, dancing nude while humming French melodies.

One night a servant, returning late to her own quarters, saw Coco dancing. Lit only by the moon, frail and magical, she seemed to float above the beds of blooming heliotrope and gardenia. The servant fell to her knees, muttering fragments of prayers and pressing her face to the ground. They found her there in the morning, affirming to have seen an angel. The news of the miracle spread in the servants' quarters and promptly found its way to the streets of the town.

Don Baldomero, unaware of the miraculous happenings in his own home, confronted the singing crowd with the serenity and aplomb inherited from his Spanish lineage. Standing at his door with crossed arms he addressed them. "So far," he said in his accented voice, "no one has informed me of such an appearance. I shall, however, investigate and reach my own conclusions, which I must tell you will be my own exclusive concern, because whether an angel lives in my house or not is my business, and you are advised to mind your own."

Mr. Fulton, taken by surprise amidst the rhapsody of his convictions, accepted the decision with exemplary humbleness and departed, followed by his proselytes.

It didn't take long for Don Baldomero to resolve the mystery of the angel. His own wife Gineviere brought Coco to his library. Always the gentleman, Don Baldomero received her with gentleness and respect.

"The past," he said in his best notarial style, "belongs to a person by natural laws. The law has established safeguards to protect a person's right to his privacy, but this legal protection is evaded by gossip and innuendo, so that while the front door to offense is closed, the back door is left open." He paused, looking at Coco with tenderness.

"Young woman," he said, stretching his hand to her, "you are now safe under my roof and protected by my honor. I ask from you that you don't look back toward your past but to your future, secure in our love. It is not good that you and Lotario start your life in adultery, so I am asking that you live separately until after your wedding."

The wedding between Coco and Lotario was performed in the house chapel by Don Bruno, the village Catholic priest. Don Bruno, a Basque from Alava, was short and *corcovado,* which is the phonetically pleasing Spanish word for hunchback. He explained his *corcova* as a mistake by God, who had started making an angel of him only to realize halfway through that he was making a man. The wings' stumps had developed into a *corcova.*

Whatever his theological shortcomings, Don Bruno was firm in faith, doubtful in hope and very strong in charity. Without questions or say-so's, he officiated at the wedding between Coco and Lotario.

After the "I do's" were exchanged, Lotario tenderly lifted his wife's veil, but his hands became frozen with horror, while a gasp of terror escaped his lips. Coco had suffered a terrible transformation. Her sweet face was now a hideous mask, with lips parted in a grimace. Kneeling with head raised like a tormented wax doll, she clutched the immobile beads of a rosary in a frozen prayer. A fly circled the flame of the alter candle. It fell awkwardly on Coco's face and walked a drunken dance, rubbing its infamy on her blue eyes.

Persons with exquisite sensitivity, when split between powerful drives that contradict each other–like hands opposing one another with equal strength–may reach a painful stalemate that immobilizes their thoughts, their emotions and even their bodies. Archaic professors called this condition "catatonia." Coco was pronounced catatonic by the village physician, who manipulated her arms, placing them in absurd positions as if she were an insensitive mannequin. Pedantically pleased with his diagnosis, he declared her incurable and departed, ignorant of her inner struggle.

In Panimache, illness as a theme of conversation follows a strict social code. *Pulmonia* and rheumatism are very well accepted; equally proper are migraine headaches, chlorosis and congestion of the liver. Malaria is regarded with doubtful reserve, as it means one is exposed to the bite of mosquitoes. Kidney malfunctions are a topic only in male company, while childbirth is reserved for feminine society. Torments of the mind are never mentioned. They imply carnal sin committed by the afflicted or by their parents–a perversion, a dishonor that stains the whole family's reputation.

Coco's diagnosis was made almost in a whisper, but secrets are not kept well in Panimache. Wine in a sieve has a better chance to be kept than gossip poured into a neighbor's ear. Soon the tale went around that Lot's wife had turned into a statue of salt in retribution for her past sins. The villagers reviewed their own lives and flocked to the church's confessional to ask absolution for their own sins, fearing, no doubt, an epidemic of catatonia. But as the days passed without other cases, the good neighbors' fickle attention trickled away to other concerns. The official announcement of an increase in the postal rate became a new source of preoccupation and the center of animated dispute at church and in the marketplace.

Coco was moved to one of the house's back quarters, separated from the everyday traffic, and was never mentioned in public. Her quarters were comfortable, even elegant, with a handsome fireplace near which she sat rigidly on a Persian rug among colorful pillows. Soon her calico cat joined her isolation. Coco accepted food from a servant, but rejected violently Lot's affection. Once when he reached for her hand she screamed and struck her head against a wall.

Don Bruno, the *corcovado* priest, came to visit daily. He sat at a distance, observing Coco with interest. He noticed her every gesture, each slight tremor in her hands, a flutter of her eyelids, the occasional painful rictus of her lips, and he waited in silence.

When life brings sadness, time is not measured in minutes or hours. Don Bruno, like a hunter of souls listening for clues, waited for the voices of his own intuition to give the signal. And so, one evening when they were alone with a woman servant, without warning or hesitation, he spoke firmly as if to himself.

"I know now," he said, "that Coco is very much like her cat. Her cat stretches and tries to leave the room, but stops, looks back at the fire that he has just left, and remains immobile–unable to decide between his two wishes."

"Yes, poor Coco is like the cat," Coco spoke.

Even though he was surprised by her sudden expression, Don Bruno continued as if nothing had happened.

"I wonder if the cat gets cramps while he waits for his mind to decide whether to go or to stay."

"The cat gets very bad cramps," said Coco with finality.

"But the cat will not let anyone rub its limbs to help the cramps," said Don Bruno. Then he added reflectively, "The cat is like I am–I won't let anyone touch my *corcova*, even though they say it brings luck, because I feel they are mocking me."

"The cat is also afraid of being hurt by love," Coco said.

"I don't blame the cat," concluded Don Bruno, "but rubbing its limbs is not love but pure medicine."

Without saying farewell, Don Bruno left. When he returned the following day, he learned that Coco had allowed the maid to wash and comb her hair and rub her swollen limbs with sweet oil.

New meetings brought gradual responses. Don Bruno had guessed that closeness frightened Coco– direct conversations were for her intolerable intrusions– yet when the comments were directed to a third person, Coco could respond to them as a child who catches a ball after it has bounced off a wall. Coco now ate by herself and helped her servant comb her lovely long hair, and she no longer kept immobile, yet she spoke of herself as if she were a third person.

"Coco is glass," she said once. "She can break like beautiful glass, and where will her soul go then?" And another time, "Do not tell Coco that she is beautiful because Coco cannot answer. What would she give in return?"

Don Bruno, careful of his every step, led her out of isolation gently like a tightrope walker showing the way to safety. He spoke of aloneness, and then he spoke of happiness, of sunrises by the sea, of mornings of freedom, galloping on a mare across the emerald fields of Navarra, of music and the simple songs of his homeland.

"If only Coco could see those fields," he said. "If only Coco could hear that music!"

"Coco hears your music," she answered, and for the first time, she smiled. She then began to speak directly to Don Bruno. Coco spoke of the vineyards of Burgundy during harvest. Her parents were farmers in Vougeot. Her life had been simple, full of light and perfumed with the air of fields in bloom. But she was young and had wished for more.

"We are brother and sister," she said. "We left home to find our dreams. They died in Panimache."

"They sleep," Don Bruno said softly.

After consulting with his bishop the priest advised the family that the wedding of Coco and Lot was invalid. Coco had been ill at the time and thus unable to receive the sacrament.

Life returned to normal at the household. Don Baldomero went back to accounts and Doña Geno to her catarrhs.

Lotario, however, wandered about disoriented, like a moth in daylight. He altered his name to Lot, took to dressing in black in the fashion of a courtier during the times of Velasquez, and paced the corridors of his house, reading aloud Goethe's *Die Leiden Des Jungen Werther*. No one guessed he intended to follow the example of the suicidal hero.

If Don Bruno had read *Thaïs* by Anatole France, he would have saved his heart much suffering. He would have learned from the monk Paphnutius that a healer always pays a price of pain for his miracles. He alone accompanied Coco to the bus station when she left Panimache to rejoin her friends. They had written about future artistic engagements in Copenhagen and Beirut.

Starry-eyed and prettier than ever, Coco left the village without a look back.

IV

SABEE

For all its beauty, Panimache is a treacherous Sea of Sargassus. Misfits from far and wide float in, unable to escape the currents, and remain in the village by the lake, wasting their lives away. I have known only one man who escaped, but he is now dead, murdered in the Mexican territory of Quintana Roo not long ago. His killer is also dead.

Sabee, as I called him, died quickly and painlessly. The killer's knife tore his heart with one single thrust. In death, his dark face was fixed in a smile of white teeth. He must have been relieved, because for a long time he had feared dying slowly, in pain and disfigurement.

No one knew him well. He was a traveling salesman who had arrived in Panimache with an attaché case full of fake jewelry that he sold from door to door. Small and dark, always smiling with large white teeth, he peddled his wares, rattling on incomprehensibly in a foreign accent, saying he came from the Punjab, which meant nothing to the people of Panimache. They called him "Sabee," imitating the Hindu word "Sahib," which he often used. Sabee was immune to rejection. He smiled his blinding white smile to the humble housewives of Panimache and, eventually, through persistence, sold them garnets that he called rubies, and green glass and opaque rhinestones, which he insisted, could pass for emeralds and diamonds.

"No one," he affirmed in his high-pitched voice, "outside of India, can tell a garnet from a ruby, and who in the village has seen a true emerald or diamond?"

I disliked Sabee and avoided his efforts to befriend me. My distaste of him was rooted in his attempt to get from me a prescription for a poison.

"For my own use, Señor Quince," he had implored. "I must have the means to escape my parents' fate, if it were to happen."

His story was sad–horrific. He had been born in a miserable village in the Punjab, of parents afflicted by leprosy. For twelve years he had lived watching in horror the pain of their physical destruction, seeing them repudiated with terror by the villagers, who feared contagion of the disease.

"I had no playmates, Señor Quince. I couldn't even kiss my mother, because her face was one infected sore."

Missionary Sisters of Saint Vincent de Paul took away the young child, and he grew up in mission houses throughout the world, ending up in Guatemala.

"Do you understand, Señor Quince? I must have a means to escape such a life. Children are infected by their parents. Perhaps even now, the disease is growing inside of me."

I thought his story was a lie–a tale to peddle misery, like his fake jewelry. I couldn't imagine such horror, so I refused his request and tried to avoid him. But, as often happens with persistent people, my rejection only increased his efforts to befriend me. Finally, I resigned myself to offering him a tolerant acceptance.

One afternoon, as I drank coffee at Al Chisme, overlooking Calle Santander, I saw Sabee carrying his attaché case. He was walking down the street that led to the Post Office, wearing black trousers, an open orange shirt and a Nehru cap. From his neck dangled a small leather bag, similar to the ones in which the *Tzutuhil* carry their totems.

"Quince!" he yelled in his high-pitched voice, upon seeing me. "Señor Quince, please take no offense from my familiarity. I have been praying for a chance to find you alone. I need to talk with you about matters of importance."

Regardless of the nuisance, one doesn't swat a bee as one does a fly.

"Sit down, Sabee," I said, offering him a chair. "Have some soda, or whatever you drink. You look like a thirsty myna bird."

"You are always ingenious in your comparisons, Señor Quince, but I take no offense."

"Maybe you should."

"I can't, because I need your help."

The sad little bird had pecked at my weakness. It is not my way to turn down someone who truly needs me.

"More poison?"

"You are very cruel, Señor Quince. No, it's not poison. I have my own poison." He glanced around to ascertain that we were alone. "Look, Señor Quince." Moving rapidly, he untied the small bag from his neck and set it on the table. As he opened it, to my horror, a small snake with black and orange rings slithered out onto the slippery Formica of the table, probing with its split tongue.

"A coral viper," I whispered, "...more poisonous than a cobra, and abundant in this land."

Rapid as a mongoose, Sabee captured the viper's head with experienced fingers and returned it to the bag.

"No, I don't need your poison, Señor Quince. She is faster, only a few seconds of pain. When the day comes, it will be more natural."

He wished for me to keep some papers in case he died.

"Are you sick now?" I asked.

"No, I check myself daily as I bathe. Each morning, I examine my body. Not a single day goes without terror."

"Not a good way to live."

"It's the only one I have known." He was not smiling now.

Strange, I thought. It is easier to find human bondage with people in sadness than through pleasure. I felt love for Sabee, for the struggle of his life, and through him I loved all men.

He opened his attaché case and brought out a manila envelope.

"My last will and testament," he said.

He put it on the table and left without a farewell, his attaché case flapping against his leg.

Two weeks later, perhaps three (my memory is no longer clear), I was notified of his death over the telephone by the Chief of Police of Corozal, in Quintana Roo. Sabee had written my name in his passport as next of kin. The Chief of Police was courteous.

"The motive for the crime was robbery," he explained. "The thief was found dead not far from the victim. Perhaps he suffered a heart attack? He was still holding an empty leather bag in which the victim must have carried his money."

"You ought to have seen..." said the chief. "A small case was broken open, and emeralds and rubies lay scattered in the mud, sparkling like one hears they do in the rivers of Brazil. Unfortunately, that night it rained and everything washed away; God knows where..."

V

THE NOVENA TO SAN MARTIN

It was an easy row back to my sloop, rocking back and forth, held by the anchor and her fate. She had started life at sea in a storm in the Caribbean waters between Tobago and Trinidad. One night a storm tore her hull against hidden rocks, and that was the end of it. A wounded boat is no longer trusted. And so, like a woman fallen into misfortune, she drifted from one master to another, until she ended up sailing the imprisoned waters of Lake Atitlan, in the highlands of Guatemala. Men and boats are ruled by fate. It took me many years to learn it.

It was four in the afternoon, the indifferent time of day before darkness. My boat rocked back and forth, held at anchor not far from shore. The people in the village were up from their siesta. One could see the women, dressed as flowers, gathered by the shore of the lake. A light breeze lifted their laughter over the water.

"Women," I said. "Without them, this village would be only a mound of dust."

Always generous with hyperbole, Uno added, "Our lives, without them, would be like the termite nests photographed in Africa by *National Geographic.*" He had been the photographer.

He stopped rowing and steadied the dingy while I secured it to my boat. I got aboard. Shortly, Uno joined me.

"Have I ever told you about Bruna?" he asked.

"Was she your lover when you lived in Mexico as a student?"

"I have told you, then! Yes, she was one of our models. She was Italian, and she photographed like a dream."

"You wrote to me in a letter: 'She has blue eyes; immense blue eyes, like sapphires hidden in the cascade of her black hair. Her breasts are small and gentle, and she has a sway back.'"

"I wish you wouldn't remember so well! She didn't have a sway back; it just seemed that way. But her voice, Quince! I have heard many lovely sounds, but none like hers. Her cadence was an invitation to adore her, and her scent was as subtle as that which orchids have when they are alive in the jungle."

"But orchids have no fragrance!"

"Some rare ones do, and she was like a rare flower, luring me to destruction. She tormented me with jealousy."

"Jealousy is a perverted form of love. Is that how you loved her?"

"No, not in the beginning, but she couldn't understand any other love."

"Was she cruel? Beautiful women often are."

"No, it was not perfidy. She feared betrayal and demanded proofs of love, but she trusted only proofs of pain. You must remember, Quince, that I was only eighteen. I had just left my father's *monterias*–his hunter's outposts in the jungle–to study photography in

Mexico and was more apt to hit a snake in the eye with a throwing knife than to understand a woman."

"You were young and ignorant," I said, smiling at a memory of my own youth.

"That, and perhaps more, but don't keep interrupting. I don't know how long my sincerity will last."

Again, I smiled to myself. "Uno, the Professor once told me 'Jealousy increases in inverse proportion to one's genitalia.' Did that apply to you?'"

"I'll need time to unravel it," replied Uno, laughing, "but what if the woman provokes the jealousy?"

"Is that what Bruna did?"

"I'm trying to tell you."

"I'll be patient. Sometimes you become baroque in your descriptions."

"Blame the times and not Spain, Quince. My memory of her still brings out the sad poet in me. She tore my heart in subtle ways. Have you heard the old saying: *'Lo que en el corazon esta a los labios se asoma?'*"

I rehearsed the Spanish refrain in my mind. It wasn't good in English: "What hides in the heart, escapes through the lips."

"Yes, I've heard it."

"Good. Now you will understand how she tormented me. As if inspired by evil harpies, after we loved–when still in a lover's embrace–she whispered questions, breathing them in my ears like drops of poison: 'Do you wish for me never to see Lorenzo? What will happen to him? Have you no pity? Have you seen his pictures for Givenchy? Why are you so jealous of poor Lorenzo?' Poor Lorenzo indeed!" Uno smiled sadly.

"Lorenzo, whose name I learned to hate, was a black man, a model like her, and he looked like a dark god! He was homosexual, but I was certain that out of vanity he would seek the conquest of Bruna, even if he could truly love only men. I had heard of such cases, but my pride prevented me from telling Bruna what I knew, and I hid my anguish from her. It's an error to admit to a woman that one fears a rival–women become curious. 'Perhaps...' they reason, 'perhaps they have missed something,' and so, their curiosity, like a scent, leads them by the nose to betrayal."

Uno rummaged in his knapsack until he found a silver flask. He shook it, listening approvingly, then reflected.

"Jealousy is one of the strangest emotions of men: the closest encounter of love and hate, of intuition and thought. It makes one deaf to reason and yet clairvoyant, like a blind man who can guess crevices, as if he could see with eyes yet undiscovered."

Suddenly, the lake turned the color of slate and shivered in the cold, like an old man in winter. It was *Xocomyl*, a violent wind that blew every afternoon, raking the peaceful waters of the lake with its fury.

Uno poured us coffee from the thermos bottle and added some brandy from his flask. The wind had brought a chill. I put on my windbreaker and went to the foredeck to check the hold of the anchor. It was firm and safe. We went down below to the cabin and sat by the map table.

"Please continue your story," I said in time.

"At the time," he obliged, "I was living at Liverpool 28 in Mexico City. It was a classic French apartment house–I don't know the name of the style–but it was solemn as an embassy, a leftover from the times of Maximilian's Empire in Mexico. In the vicinity there were many similar homes. The neighborhood had known better times, and now maintained an air of impoverished aristocracy. Blanche from *A Streetcar Named Desire* would have felt at home. The place was well-known among students as an excellent boarding house. The rooms, many of which had been servants' quarters, were kept very clean, and the food was rich and abundant. The owners of the house were twins–*Las Señoritas del Castillo*–identical in appearance, but totally different in character from each other, as if shuffled together by accident.

"Lupita and Fernandita, the twins, made Liverpool 28 what it was. Fernandita was in charge of collecting the rents. She supervised the servants that cleaned the place, and set the standards of dress and behavior in the house. She seldom smiled–her pretty face was wasted like a flower in a vase. She was a specimen of extended maidenhood, not to be interrupted by romantic nonsense. Her sensuous figure, punished by corsets and restraints, was destined one day to wilt without ever knowing the temptations of passion. Her hair was disciplined into a bun, and at the sound of her clipped, high-heeled steps, we straightened our postures and checked our ties. She had renounced sin in favor of her twin sister, who looked like a dissipated cousin. Lupita's rich auburn hair was always in glorious disarray; her green eyes were sleepy and she moved uncertainly, like a cat in the early morning. Gliding through the kitchen, her sultry figure wrapped in a Japanese kimono, she tasted with a quick, dipping finger this or that, smiling to the servants, who revered her as a goddess.

"Some of the oldest maids, who had known the twins when they were infants, gossiped that their mother, who was from Paraguay, had nursed them each from a separate breast. One of her breasts gave sweet milk while the other was sour as vinegar. 'She hadn't meant any harm,' they whispered. 'She had been born that way.'"

Uno smiled and shrugged his shoulders. He poured himself another cup of coffee and one for me. Then he shook the brandy flask, pouring a generous shot into both our cups. "But to get back to Bruna—I was losing my self-respect, and becoming a snoop. Many nights I walked the streets where she lived with my eyes riveted to the window of her apartment, guessing her doings. It was mad irony. I sought to surprise her in some betrayal, and yet prayed for her innocence.

"One night, as I walked her street under a drizzle, I noticed a light at her place on the third floor. Before I knew what I was doing I had reached first a tree branch, then the iron of a window, and then climbed the empty walls, finding handholds where no one would think any existed. My hunter's training in the jungle was paying off. She was alone, walking from one place to another, dropping her earrings at her boudoir and a scarf and gloves on a chair, magical as she moved with the freedom of innocence, discarding the thousand and one things a woman has to discard. Every so often, she peered into the darkness of the window, as if she could guess. Her apprehension filled me with perverted excitement."

Uno moved his head, reproving himself.

"Of all the sins a man can inflict on a woman, voyeurism is the easiest to forgive," I said. "If only...," I mused, "if only we could live solely by instinct, like tigers!"

I reached for Uno's shoulder in a comforting gesture.

I knew how tigers hunted. I had seen a jaguar lying on a tree limb. She was stalking a doe, intense and immobile, but for electric ripples in her velvety tail. Suddenly, the doe broke into a fugue-like dance, not knowing what she was escaping from, her desperate leaps loosing her into the green jungle. Up on the limb, the jaguar closed her eyes and lowered her beautiful head into her paws.

"Bruna went into another room where I couldn't see her," Uno continued. "I was holding precariously to some small projections on the wall outside her window, so I made myself safer by reaching for the branch of an acacia tree that grew close by. The view to her place changed, so I could now see a part of her bathroom. She was taking a bath. I gazed upon her through the glass. She looked like a pensive nymph rubbing the soles of her feet with a sponge–a private moment stolen for all time to play over in my mind. That was all I saw, an innocent moment, and yet that brief vision sufficed to defeat me."

"Why?" I asked, even though I knew the answer.

"I lost my self-respect," Uno said, his handsome face accented by the sadness of his eyes. "I had photographed her nude. Posing was her job. I had loved her; it was her gift to me. But now I had taken from her all she had left–her solitude. I was a thief out of the dark, and I knew I had been cursed."

"I understand," I said, "but the gods who curse can also forgive."

Speaking slowly in his raspy voice, Uno said, "Guilt is a useless sentiment, but it bites into one's soul like a viper and drains one's will to live."

"But you survived!"

"Yes, I survived that terrible night I fell from grace. As I went home, the old streets which I had walked thousands of times were now haunted dark alleys, losing me, mocking my steps with unfamiliar echoes, echoes of following vampires, darkness drinking in the absinthe light of drunken lampposts. I felt the anguish of Eve and of Adam, their ears still hearing the terrible voice of their creator condemning them to a life without hope, afar from gentle bounty, earning their bread with sweat and bearing their children in pain! What were the thoughts of our parents while huddling together in the cold night? Did they hold one another and breathe love into each other's lips? Or did they thrust their anguish into desperate passion, in an embrace of hate, to procreate Cain?"

Uno paused. Then he spoke softly, like someone reading in a dim light.

"The rain had ceased when I reached Liverpool 28. It was already dawn. The iron gate was ajar. In the beginning light, I recognized Lupita, her figure gliding through the enclosed garden. Lupita, the enchantress. At the sounds of my steps on the gravel she turned in alarm, her hand to her throat. Then she recognized me. 'My God!' she whispered. 'You are destroyed.'

"She came close to me and posed her hand on my forehead. I was shivering with cold. My arms and chest hurt and my head spun madly, like a broken carousel. Under her touch, my strength failed. I forgot to breathe, and my body fell to the ground."

Uno stopped talking. He got up, and, from a drawer, he pulled out a striped pullover, which I recognized.

"I got that in Biarritz!" I exclaimed. Uno spoke, but his voice was muffled by the cloth as he slipped my sweater over his head.

"*El Doctor* Casimiro Dubois had trained in Paris," he repeated. "He was a round man, with a pale face and a balding head. He dressed like a dandy, and pronounced 'R's' as if he were gargling. The *Señoritas del Castillo* had called him to examine me, but he couldn't decide whether I had suffered pneumonia from exposure to the rain or nervous exhaustion with fever. He doubted if I would survive. He wasn't reckoning with the miracles of San Martin de Porras.

"Now, as saints go, San Martin is a minimal one," Uno explained. "He was a Negro born in Peru, who joined the Dominicans after other religious orders refused him. In that congregation, he was assigned insignificant tasks, such as sweeping the dust from corridors and cells. The younger monks called him *Fray escoba*, which meant 'Friar broom.' He would fly into mystic ecstasies for hours at a time, standing in a trance with his broom uselessly dangling from his hands. The cleaning in his monastery was left to mice and birds. As a miraculous healer, however, his fame spread far and wide through the land. He was the saint to whom Lupita commended my recovery, and, as a healer, he ran circles around *El Doctor* Casimiro Dubois. After nine days my fever disappeared, and even though I was still weak, my life was no longer in danger.

"My room was small and crowded. Most of the space was taken by my bed, which was made of heavy carved wood and had a matching side table, bearing pictures of my family, a candlestick of copper and an alarm clock. The walls were adorned with photographs of houses and nudes. A desk occupied the rest of the room. Lupita had built on it a small altar with a plaster effigy of a little Negro holding a broom. A candle burned in front of the image. Even though he had rescued me when I was on the borders of death, I resented the devotion with which Lupita prayed to the black saint and felt that, like Lorenzo, St. Martin was stealing my woman." Uno shrugged his shoulders in a gesture that he wore like an old jacket.

"The truth is that I had no claim whatsoever on Lupita, but it's the nature of youth to invent passions and tragedies, and so I had built a romance around Lupita's gentle care of me during my illness. For nine evenings she brought my dinner and waited while I swallowed thick and savory soups. She would then clear my improvised bed table, and while I sipped robust Burgundy, she engaged me in conversation, probing gently, like a lover disrobing my soul. Under the spell of her words my memories of Bruna gradually became faint, like an old photograph in its silver frame, while Lorenzo's gladiator image was replaced by the gentle continence of Martin's miracle, or my heart capitulating to Lupita's explanations.

"'Jealousy,' Lupita said, 'is the cry of a child enamored with a goddess who ignores his passion.' A child, she reasoned, was only a child, incapable of passions."

"How wrong!" I interrupted. "Passion is the essence of childhood."

Uno agreed. "As Lupita explained this mystery to me, I relived the anguish I experienced when my brother Domingo was born. Do you remember Domingo?"

"Vaguely," I said.

"When he was born I was kept away from him," said Uno, "because seeing him made me ill. I refused to eat, cried without reason, and at night suffered terrible nightmares. They feared for my life. The family physician was of no help, and, in despair, my parents followed sage advice of an Indian servant and prepared *una Fiesta de Angeles*."

"A feast for angels?" I asked.

"Yes. It is a pagan ceremony with religious overtones. Children dressed like angels are treated to a breakfast of delicious sweets, cakes, pastries and exquisite refreshments, all served by their mothers. After their appetite is satisfied, the host child makes one wish, which must be fulfilled."

"It must have worked for you," I said, smiling.

"Not fully," laughed Uno. "I asked that Domingo be painted black and thrown into the river!"

"Poor Domingo!" I said. "What did they do?"

"They made a doll of blackened beeswax; the village priest pretended to baptize it with the name Domingo, and we all marched with music and firecrackers and dumped it into the river!"

"And you got well?" I asked.

"I got well," said Uno, "until my relapse with Bruna." Uno poured what was left of the brandy into our coffee.

"One can never second guess life, least of all in matters of the heart." He spoke thoughtfully. Then in a lighter tone he added, "I mean no disrespect, Quince, and I am no expert in theology, but I am convinced that saints often find themselves beyond their depth. Maybe they are still apprentices, and in their eagerness to answer prayers they act rashly. This is an imponderable. What is palpable is that their miracles often turn out to be enormous catastrophes!"

"But San Martin cured you!"

"I am not denying that he is an excellent healer, but I doubt his character. Behind his benign demeanor he hides an inclination toward mischief. But it will be better if you judge this for yourself. The last night of the Novena, I waited for Lupita to come as she had done every night. Instead a servant brought my meal, which I barely touched, dismissing her promptly. Reclining in my bed, I drank my wine slowly and in a daze thought about her, repeating the verse King Solomon sang while he waited for Sheba:

Return, return, O maid of Shulam
Return, return, that we may gaze on you!
How beautiful are your feet in their sandals,
The curve of your thighs is like the curve of a
necklace worked by a master hand
Your navel is a bowl well rounded
With no lack of wine, your belly a heap of wheat
Surrounded with lilies
Your two breasts are like two fawns,
Twins of a gazelle.

"The door opened, and Lupita entered my room. She was covered lightly by veils of silk, like an odalisque painted by Delacroix. She smiled, perhaps delighted by my confusion. Silently, she stood in the flickering light of the votive candle that burned in front of the saint, and slowly let her veils fall, revealing her immaculate body. Her proud head was held by a delicate neck. Her breasts moved with the rhythm of her breathing. The gentle slope of her navel guided my eyes to the secret of Venus, guarded by amber thighs. Nude as she was, she genuflected in front of San Martin, and then walked toward me.

> *In stature like a palm tree,*
> *Its fruit clusters her breasts...*

"I will climb the palm tree, I resolved; I will seize its cluster of dates.

"She loved me that night, and on the night that followed, and every time we loved, she was a new woman in her love.

"Two mornings I awoke wrapped in her perfumed scent. On the third morning, Angela, the oldest servant, brought a note from Fernandita asking me to vacate my room by the end of the month–three days hence. The note invited me to come to the sisters' quarters that evening at seven, and to bring with me the image of San Martin.

"Their apartment was on the highest floor of the house, and if I hadn't been in such anguish, I would have delighted at its exquisite decor. Angela let me in and went to advise the sisters of my arrival. In spite of my pain I marveled at the view, from a wide French window, of the two magical volcanoes that guard the city of Mexico, Ixtacihuatl, the sleeping woman, her sensuous form sculpted in snow, and Popocatepetl. In the setting sun she was painted with the soft hues of early womanhood, contrasting with the darker tones of her warrior lover. I thought of broken fragments of a poem by Ramon Lopez Velarde:

Suave Patria, vendedora de chía,
quiero raptarte en la cuaresma opaca,
sobre un grañón y con matgraca
y entre los tiros de la policia.'

"I tried to remember more, but my thoughts were interrupted by Lupita, dressed in a lovely pale yellow kimono. She greeted me, kissing me on both cheeks.

"'My sister will be here shortly,' she breathed. 'Poor Uno, I am afraid we have created a disaster. Did you bring San Martin?'"

"I gave her the image of the saint, which I had wrapped in a silk kerchief. She set it on a table and spoke to him reproachfully."

"'Ungrateful saint,' she said. 'I had been warned of your twisted humor. It doesn't matter now, but don't expect me to again be your devotee. You have heard the last of my novenas!'"

"Her rambling was interrupted when the door opened and–I couldn't believe my eyes–I saw again Lupita entering the room, dressed in a pale pink kimono. Like her sister, she kissed me on both cheeks, and led me to a divan. I was feeling faint. The twins sat on low chairs, facing me."

"'Now you understand why you must leave,' said Lupita in pink.

"'It was all an error, not in bad faith, but an error nevertheless,' said Lupita in yellow. 'We both nursed you. When one tired, the other took her place. But we didn't count on our passions and ended, both of us, making love with you without the knowledge by the other.'"

"But, who was first?" I demanded.

"Lupita dressed in pink raised her hand. 'I was, but there is no need for explanations. Go now, and take this funny little saint with you. After all, he did you a good turn.'"

"I couldn't resist laughing. The sisters also laughed. It was a sad laugh. We embraced and kissed when I left, with the saint under my arm."

"Strange story," I said. "And Bruna? Did you go back to her?"

"My heart had guessed the truth all along. I received a letter from her, posted in Venezuela. She and Lorenzo had left Mexico together to open a dancing studio in Maracaibo."

VI

A BASKET OF CRABS

It was morning, and the lake was sapphire blue. The lake was always blue in the morning. We were lying at anchor in *El Termometro Feliz*, not far from shore but far enough away from the peddlers, children and their dogs, and women prattling and selling their tempting poisonous food.

I was welding two thin wires in the shape of an elongated cross. Uno was sitting on the foredeck, sipping a beer, wearing khaki shorts without a shirt, and his ears were painted green. He had returned the previous night from photographing rare birds for the National Geographic Society. On his last night in the jungle, he had sprayed himself with what he thought was insect repellent, only to find out it was camouflage-green paint. His employers from the National Geographic Society called him "Emilio Green Ears" and joyfully gave him a bonus in exchange for a photograph that they labeled: "Our guide, Emilio Orejas Verdes."

"I went to the same school with this guy." Uno's voice was hoarse, as if he had a cold.

"Which guy?" I asked.

"The guy who makes this beer." He took a sip. "We called him 'Cabro' as a nickname–we thought he didn't have it up there," Uno said, tapping his head. "But he turned the joke on us."

"Why did you call him 'Cabro'?"

"He looked like a billy goat. Now the label of his beer is a laughing goat, laughing with good reason: he's made millions."

Uno crushed his empty can and dropped it in the box where we keep crumpled cans. He and I had grown up together, better than brothers. I called him Uno, even if his true name was Emilio. He was a jungle guide and nature photographer, but he was more; he was a healer and some said a *brujo*, a man who had secret dealings with forces of the occult. The military distrusted him because he spoke the language of the Indians, who loved him and trusted his advice, but the guerrillas, for the same reasons, feared him.

"So you're still intent on betting on your madness?" he asked.

"I'll raise the bet," I answered.

"Two pesos for each crab?"

"Make it five." Then I changed my mind. "Leave it at two, a limit of fifty crabs."

I had bet with Uno that I could fish for crabs and catch them by the eye. I had learned the trick from an old fisherman on the Hawaiian island of Molokai and didn't want to take too much of Uno's money.

I finished making my crab container, a frame made of thin wire in the shape of a cross with arms of equal length. A thread of fine fishing line was tied around the frame to form a rhombus. This was affixed to a long, thin bamboo pole. When one looped the eye of a crab, it closed his eye horizontally against its shell, trapping the thread and tightening the grip as irritation increased. One could then easily lift the crab by the eye and shake it into a bucket. Not too kind a procedure, granted, but sportier than luring them with food into a trap.

We rowed the dingy to the shallows of Tzanjuyu, where on the flat white rocks napped hundreds of crabs. I lassoed thirty-seven of the largest and could have caught more, but felt sorry for Uno, who winced as if it were him I was yanking by the eye.

We sat under a tree, wondering what to do with the crabs. Then a *Tzutuhil* woman, carrying a child on her back wrapped in her *rebezo*, appeared from nowhere, silent and secretive like any other living thing from the wild. A few steps behind her, following in her tracks, a boy of four or five years old carried on his back a minimal load of sticks and moss.

"*Buenos dias, Tata*," she said.

"*Buenos dias, Nana*," I answered.

"*Buenos dias, Tata*," she said to Uno.

"*Buenos dias, Nana*."

She stood there silently, watching the bucket with the crabs. Her little son rested his load of sticks with much noise and doings, as he had seen men in his tribe do. Crouched near them, he waited.

She spoke then in *Tzutuhil*, facing Uno, not me, as if she had guessed he would understand. The short phrases were clipped and raspy, like clearing of the throat.

"She wants to buy the crabs," Uno said.

"Tell her they are hers. I'm giving them to her and her boy."

"What about the bet?" Uno asked.

"I've proven my point. Let's make them happy for one day."

"*Vale!*" said Uno. He then spoke to the woman in *Tzutuhil*.

The woman started a fire, and, as if conjured by the smoke, her young husband appeared, smiling. He was dressed in the colors of his tribe–purple stripes on a white blouse, and trousers that reached to his knee. His head was covered by a purple tsute. He had been cutting reeds that grew abundantly in this part of the lake. He was a basket weaver from San Juan la Laguna, a village high above the lake. He sharpened little green branches from a guava tree, with which he stabbed the crabs one at a time, carefully roasting them over the open fire like marshmallows. His wife had meanwhile prepared a *chirmolito*, a hot sauce with green tomatillo and hot peppers sprinkled with coarse salt, and unwrapped tortillas that she carried in banana leaves. It was a good meal, eaten in peace and good faith.

There were still many crabs left, and the woman carefully arranged them in her basket. They seemed to be praying, their claws raised to heaven like religious supplicants.

A small green lizard darted from the ground to the edge of the basket, her onyx eyes measuring distances. After two miniature-stretching efforts, she jumped, but fell short into what suddenly became a brutal, tearing and ripping mob that destroyed her limb-by-limb, tail, head and eyes, with ugly movements of jaws and obscene swallowing, until there was nothing left.

A cold wind blew suddenly from the lake, and with it a fleeting memory, a name: Catalina...

Florecita was not her name; that was just what I called her. Her name was Catalina. I learned about love with her one evening when the grownups were away. She accepted me shyly, offering her small breasts, like unripe fruit, and her beginning womanhood timidly, as if expecting pain. I loved her not only with my body, but sensed a part of me joining her nature, as we breathed the same air in a kiss. She was an Indian girl, forbidden to me by my religion.

On a Friday, I confessed to Father Pablo, the Dominican priest, who heard me in hard silence. From the darkness of his confessional he demanded that I repent.

But I couldn't.

Visions of eternal fire and damnation crossed my eyes. Without absolution my soul was lost–condemned to an eternity of grief, excommunicated, no longer a participant in the mysteries of Eucharist, barred from the company of angels, anathema, a child with a damned soul.

And still I couldn't repent.

Desperate, I described her copper figure, the rising of her nubile breasts and frightened nipples, the soft caress of her incipient puberty.

"Could you repent," I asked in anguish, "if she had loved you?"

The priest gasped in horror. "A vampire...a demon!" he hissed, spreading his hand in front of my eyes. "*Detente*, go into the darkness from where thou came!"

Month after month on each first Friday, I returned to the confessional in despair, fearing eternal damnation, and every time I was sent away because I didn't repent.

One day, I heard Catalina had died in secret, unattended childbirth...

The *Xocomyl* started to blow. It was the wind that agitated the waters of the lake every afternoon. The

Tzutuhil woman covered the crabs with moist banana leaves. Then she nursed her baby, wrapped him in her *rebozo* and tied him to her back. She lifted the basket and balanced it on her head. Her older child gathered his sticks and moss, and her man loaded his reeds. With a gentle gesture of farewell they left through the jungle paths only they could see.

Uno and I, with our memories, again sailed away.

VII

THE PROPHET

The plaza of Jaripitio had never looked prettier, not even when it was first inaugurated ten years before. The trees, which were then saplings, had grown to splendid maturity, with green foliage dotted by birds, and the parquets had flowers in glorious disarray, tended mainly by nature. Children and dogs ran freely, as if they had also sprouted from the soil. In the center of the plaza, in a pavilion pointed like a sombrero, six or seven musicians passionately blew into their trombones and horns to an audience of wide-eyed peasants, dressed in white cotton trousers and loose blouses, holding their straw hats as though in church. Scattered here and there, small tables offered candy wrapped in papers of many colors, combs, hair pins, soaps and small bottles of perfume with names like "Noche de Luna en Venezia" or "Rapture of Love in Tahiti," which evoked distant lands and romance. A small carousel circled, propelled by youngsters hired for the job, with a few children sitting unsmiling astride tiny dog-like horses. A man, surrounded by little pink clouds of sugar affixed to a pole, walked around selling cotton candy.

In a corner, almost hidden, a small man dressed in blue serge stood leaning on a crutch behind a tiny table covered in green velvet. A group of younger peasants, the girls all ribbons and giggles, the boys hiding behind each other with backslaps and elbow thrusts, listened to him.

"What are we?" he demanded in a deep-timbred voice, "but scattered leaves of the book of life...incomplete chapters of the great novel...aware only of the few pages that we read as we go from cradle to sepulcher?" He paused and coughed into a blue bandana. Bleeding again he thought, as he saw his spit. He wished he had brought his red kerchief; it hid the blood better.

Looking into the eyes of his audience, he exclaimed, "Oh! How many errors, how many terrible mistakes, how many tears we could spare our poor selves if we could only know what is written in the next chapter!"

The audience had grown and now listened with increasing awe. "What price would we not pay for such knowledge?" the man asked dramatically. "Now, with the help of invisible great seers of the past, an innocent bird will reveal some of those hidden secrets, for fifty *centavos*, in advance."

With great care he brought out from below a small bundle, which he set on the table. It contained a cage from which a small gray bird with a helmet-like black head and white markings below its eyes chirped contentedly. It was a Java sparrow, not a bird from the region, given to him by an American tourist who had to depart suddenly, leaving behind Louis Rice, her pet bird.

Flaminio Alterio, better known by his nickname "Minio," had been born in Abruzzi, his mother's homeland. An accident of fortune had brought his mother from eastern Italy to Jaripitio in central Mexico, where she–a young widow left with child by Don

Vincenzo Alterio–remarried Paco Gonzales, an itinerant photographer. She died in childbirth, and Minio was brought up by his stepfather, who gave him a childhood sprinkled with the art of making a living at the expense of the naive.

As a child, he accompanied his photographer stepfather to the many town fairs where Paco Gonzales took pictures of weddings, baptisms and funerals, while Minio learned to pick pockets from Eusebio Diaz, one of his father's friends who specialized in that art.

For a few years he also served as an apprentice to a magician who charged one peso each to a perplexed audience for a sight of John the Baptist's head, decapitated at the request of Salome. The head was Minio's. It was covered by a black cloth and rested in a platter placed on the top of a table with a false bottom for his small frame to hide in. The magician's daughter, Rosalinda, played Salome. A pretty girl of fourteen, dressed in yellow trousers and a red vest, Rosalinda danced to the rhythm of Ravel's Bolero, allowing in her violent gyrations glimpses of incipient brown breasts. The dance culminated with Salome snatching away the black cloth revealing the Baptist's head on the platter. With tears flowing she would kiss its lips, saying, "Forgive me, my little prophet." To spectators' amazement, the head opened its eyes, declaiming in a cavernous tone, "'*Te perdono, hermana*'." The drama ended with those forgiving words, and the peasants drifted away with tears in their eyes.

It had rained many times since those early years, and many years had passed since he had last visited Jaripitio. As he grew older, Minio no longer fit into the false bottom of the table and was fired from his job. He left, taking Rosalinda with him. Both youngsters found work at a traveling circus where, because of his natural agility, he was hired as an apprentice tightrope walker while Rosalinda, prettily dressed as a ballerina, sold balloons and candy at the circus entrance.

Towns followed towns in a kaleidoscope of bliss for the lovers. But young love is always doomed. It ended suddenly when Minio fell from a tightrope and broke his hip. The circus moved on without him and Rosalinda went with it, now under the protection of the trapeze man. Minio never saw her again. He avoided circuses as he dragged himself with the help of a crutch from fair to fair, reading palms or laying the cards of tarot. He was an old man at age thirty, his lungs weakened by tuberculosis, breathing only enough air to keep him alive without a purpose, with hardly a dream. He trained the little bird after changing its name to Camarada. He liked the sound of the word, which he had first heard at a political rally of the National Communist Party. The bird was now a proletarian, a wage earner.

"For fifty *centavos* my magic bird Camarada will tell your fortune and give you advice for a happy future," he announced. "Any takers? How about you, distinguished young lady?" he asked a middle-aged woman, who walked away offended. "You, handsome young gentleman?" speaking to a youngster, who shuffled from one foot to another and then timidly paid his fifty cents.

"Camarada," Minio said, speaking to the bird, "ask your benefactors to inspire you to tell the good fortune for the gentleman." He opened a box with folded papers of different colors, which he spread on the table. He then opened the cage door, and the pretty bird hopped out.

"Will you ring a wedding bell for the young gentleman?" He set on the table a diminutive bell that the bird took in its beak, making it ring.

"And will you pull a wedding cart for the young gentleman?" he asked again, harnessing Camarada to a small cart which the bird pulled with jerky movements.

"Well done, Camarada. Now please choose for him a little paper with his fortune."

The bird picked a folded green paper which it then offered to the young man, hopping back to its cage to be rewarded by Minio with a few seeds while the youngster walked away to read his fortune in secrecy.

A woman dragging a fat child by the hand had joined the group.

"Be quiet, Pepe," she said to the child, jerking him by the arm. "You will frighten the pretty bird." Her voice was firm but lacked conviction, and its cadence startled Minio. It echoed in his heart, bringing tears to his eyes. He felt the touch of her eyes like the fingers of someone blind trying to recognize a face. He pulled the brim of his hat to hide his tears, to hide himself. No, it couldn't be her. It had been...what, fifteen years? Time's not the same when one is happy. When one is dead, there is no time.

"I want the little bird!" the child whined impertinently.

"I want... I want this... I want that... Do you know any other words? Spoiled *escuincle*!" She had used the popular word for brats.

"And why shouldn't he have it, if he wants it?" The question came from a big man, half-muscular, half-obese, and dressed in the uniform of captain of police. His voice was loud, acrid like the smell of gunpowder.

"Isn't he my son? Why shouldn't he have what he wants? I ask you–why shouldn't he?"

"The bird belongs to the man," the woman answered timidly. "It's his magic bird, his little prophet."

"Prophet, my eye!" laughed the man. "Didn't you notice how he tapped on the table to tell the bird what to do? Like Morse code. Some prophet. He is just one more scammer out of some ambulant circus." He looked at her with evil intent. "Of all people, you should know!" Approaching Minio, "How much?" he asked, pulling out a leather bag brimming with silver pesos.

"It's not for sale. The Señora is right; the bird is a prophet."

"I didn't ask if it was for sale." The man's voice was dry. "Thirty silver pesos. Isn't that the going rate for prophets?"

He started counting the silver pesos on the table.

"No!" yelled Minio in despair. "*Nunca!*" he said, terrified by the temptation. The strain provoked a fit of coughing. He brought his bandanna to his mouth and felt the warmth of blood oozing through his fingers. With his free hand he opened the cage's door. The bird came out, his head cocked, trying to understand.

"Escape, Camarada!" Minio screamed, banging on the table with an open hand.

The bird sensed the anguish of the man. It flew away. It flew until it was only a dot in the air, then it disappeared in the light.

"*Adios*, Camarada. *Hasta la vista. Ciao...*" Minio tried to say some words of farewell, anything to hear his own voice, but he couldn't, because of his cough.

VIII

THE TREASURE OF DON FIDELIO

Alizarin was a sincere artist. He baked bread to eke out a living, occasionally sold a painting, and invariably spent all his money on canvases and oils. He was French, from Saint Jean de Luz. Young looking at age fifty-four, steel-gray haired and hazel-eyed, he smiled often but took everything with the utmost seriousness. He painted volcanoes. Guatemala, with forty-two of them, was his promised land.

His home, built of adobe on the outskirts of Panimache, was whitewashed clean with windows painted Mediterranean blue and a door framed by ivy. He decorated it combining its colors and textures with the same attention he paid to his paintings. To enter his house was like stepping into a canvas. At first one walked lightly, as if afraid of smearing the paint.

The house was reached by crossing a wooden bridge, which was often under water during the rainy season when the river grew high. His few visitors, stripped to underwear, waded across the water knowing they would be comforted on arrival with glasses of hot lemonade spiced with cinnamon, ginger and brandy.

Perhaps that's why Don Fidelio turned up one rainy evening after supper. Don Fidelio, among other things, was an alcoholic.

The meal–in celebration of Alizarin's sale of a painting–was fun, but laborious to prepare. The river had been running high and swift, carrying in its current a great number of crayfish. Alizarin had rigged a simple trap of woven reeds and caught several pounds of them.

Two weeks before, I had received from him a formal, hand written invitation, listing a menu:

Menu Chez Alizarin
Chalmette oyster soup
Omellete sans nom per Alice B. Toklas
White rice with green peas
Langue a la mode du Paix Basque
Salad Aphrodite
Dulce. Café. Cigars.

He had mixed words in a colorful phonetic salad, but I knew what a splendid cook he was and had reciprocated to the invitation by sending ahead half a case of Chilean red table wine. Promising as the menu read, I was pleasantly surprised when I arrived at his home and found it changed. He had covered the circular wooden table of his studio with newspapers. In the center, he set an old iron cauldron replete with lovely pink crayfish boiled in a Cajun broth with little morsels of sausage. Two green candles set in black bottles distorted our shadows, while his old gramophone played *Pagliacci*.

The music, with frequent scratches–relics of many playings–blended with the faint smell of turpentine and the sensual bouquet of the wine.

Supper finished, we sat by the fire to sip cognac.

"Of all the operas, not one moves me as *Pagliacci*," I said.

"You are not alone. It encompasses the whole tragedy of humanity."

"Who is Polychinelle in our lives?"

"Tonio? It is a tragic being who distorts our realities. He changes plays into tragedies.

"Could Polychinelle be a woman?" I asked.

Alizarin seemed pained. "Please," he said, "let's not speak of women. Let's play the opera again."

Once more, the tired gramophone scratched the *Pagliacci* prologue and then we heard Cannio ask:

"*Me accordan de parlar?*"

"*Hola, alguien en casa?*" A baritone voice interrupted the music.

Alizarin stopped the gramophone, carefully restored the record to its cardboard envelope, and went to the door to let in the unexpected visitor. A man of fine appearance, bald and prematurely aged by a life of dissipation, Don Fidelio had a weakness for alcohol, long words, and the occult. He had a pleasant voice that had earned him the position of General Service Officer at the local chapter of Alcoholics Anonymous. He owned the only homeopathic pharmacy in the village, La Bienhechora, which advertised drugs with exaggerated therapeutic claims.

Don Fidelio was soaking wet. He had waded across the river and now coughed forcibly while tucking his shirttails inside his trousers. He had left his wet shoes and socks by the door, and now walked gingerly on his white bare feet, as if the floor were strewn with needles. Alizarin promptly brought him a towel with which he dried his bald head and face, while his eyes darted around the room.

"Bisquit?" he asked, appraising the bottle of cognac. "Very rare–haven't seen a bottle in centuries."

Alizarin delayed his offering.

"Would you enjoy some hot lemonade?" he asked.

"Something stronger, if you please." Don Fidelio eyed the bottle lovingly. "Yes, in my humble opinion Bisquit is superior to Remy Martin, not to speak of Courvoisier, and yet you seldom find it anymore."

"I heard they have gone out of business," Alizarin said.

"God forbid!" Don Fidelio seemed genuinely terrified. Alizarin brought a snifter and poured generously.

"Drink slowly," he advised. "The rain seems to be here to stay, and I have nothing else left."

Don Fidelio sniffed, tasted and bent his head like a devout Catholic receiving communion.

"I don't savor cognac too often," he explained.

"Cognac is expensive," I offered.

Don Fidelio smiled condescendingly.

"Price is no object to me. We in the apothecary business are often given gifts and gratuities by our providers. Spirits...perfumes...*en fin*, the products we retail."

"Laxatives?" inquired Alizarin.

"I meant little samples...like the small bottles one gets in the airplanes, not that I drink them. I am a recovering alcoholic. Every so often I have wine with my meals, but I boil it first in the microwave, you know..." he looked at me as if I were his accomplice, "to burn the alcohol off."

"You better not try and microwave the cognac," said Alizarin. "Quince would microwave you."

Don Fidelio turned to me with apprehension.

"As a matter of fact, I was hoping to interest Quince in a problem that I face."

He waited with pleading eyes fixed on me.

"A problem? I hope it's not conjugal; I don't care for conjugal problems."

"I am not that fortunate. I live alone, and, until recently, shared my home with my uncle Casimiro, my father's older brother, who passed away some three months ago."

Don Fidelio took a measured sip from his drink.

"Do you think drinking this little cognac will annul my sobriety?" he asked of no one. "I have now been sober for ninety-two days.

He didn't wait for an answer. He took a longer sip while glancing at the bottle, calculating its contents.

"Drinking is only an occasional problem for me. Unfortunately, the night my uncle died I had indulged and didn't have all my wits. Why with the anguish and mourning...if a man can't have a drink under those circumstances, what kind of a man is he?"

He looked at us as if expecting a challenge.

"So," I said, "you were drunk when your uncle died. What is your problem now?"

"My problem has spilled over. My uncle–may his soul rest in peace–was a bit of a miser. He didn't trust banks, or anyone for that matter. During his illness, I waited on him night and day until the day when, sensing he was going away, he told me where he had buried his savings."

Don Fidelio looked sadly at his empty glass and turned his eyes to Alizarin.

"The problem is that because of my condition I forgot what my uncle said."

Even though I lived in a village where the bizarre was frequent, Don Fidelio's predicament amused me, and I couldn't speak for fear of bursting into laughter.

"What do you want us to do?" Alizarin asked.

"I thought maybe I could ask you to assist with a little experiment. I mean no offenses, nor do I doubt your intellectual integrity, but I wonder if you could assist me by interrogating the Ouija board. It requires three persons, and frankly I don't trust the discretion of the members of A.A., who are the only other persons I know."

And that is how, two days later, Alizarin and I found ourselves at Don Fidelio's home, sitting in a darkened living room with our hands lightly posed on a triangular little board, which darted to the alphabet printed on the Ouija Board, pointing to letters until it spelled a name–Doña Milagritos–and told us that the lady *quien murio en forma tragica* was going to guide us to the discovery of a very great fortune.

Doña Milagritos, in spite of her "tragic death", which she didn't clarify, had preserved her delightful sense of humor. For the next three weeks she directed us to excavate first in one room and then in another, until Don Fidelio's house looked like a battle-scarred field with trenches dug in each of them to the depth of four feet.

Doña Milagritos affirmed that "in the world of the unseen, errors occur due to interference by *fuerzas burlonas y seductoras.*"

With aching muscles from digging, I withdrew from the séances, deciding I had heard enough from the "mocking and seductive forces." I suspected Don Fidelio was afflicted with *Mal de Piedra*, a strange ailment which leads men to dig for treasures all of their lives, squandering their fortunes in the search. They are ruled by this obsession, which is deaf to reason and immune to threats or entreaties. Women also are often afflicted, and I had heard of one instance where a luxurious house was reduced to shambles because the lady owner kept knocking down walls.

For two months Don Fidelio, assisted by Alizarin, excavated his home, his yard and the sidewalk of his home without finding the promised treasure. He was then directed by Doña Milagritos to excavate underneath the confessional at the Church of Perpetual Help, which was hesitantly permitted by the priest after Don Fidelio donated a new organ to the church.

This excavation was fruitless. How long he would have continued digging is only a matter of speculation. Doña Milagritos urged more excavations and he obeyed blindly. No place was sacred or safe from his diggings until the day when she ordered them to excavate Alizarin's living room. Alizarin was adamant in his refusal.

Doña Milagritos insinuated that this was motivated by his own plan to excavate and keep the treasure for himself. Angrily, Alizarin refused to participate any longer in the séances, and in retaliation Doña Milagritos refused to dictate one more word.

Don Fidelio, despondent as a betrayed lover, sat in front of his mute board for many days and nights, shivering as if preyed upon by malaria.

Finally, the authorities removed him, fearing for his life. In lieu of any facilities for cases like his, with regrets and apologies he was locked in a cell at the local jail.

Feverish, miserable and tormented, with hollowed eyes, hungry and unshaven, Don Fidelio could have remained in jail for the rest of his life, but for the earthquake on the second of February, which demolished his cell. The whole jail collapsed, and prisoners ran off singing praises to Providence while their guards, overwhelmed by the portent, watched passively. Don Fidelio's cell sank into the crevice and he was feared dead.

When the dust settled, however, to the surprise of authorities and villagers, out came Don Fidelio triumphantly holding a Pre-Columbian statuette of gold. The providential finding of a burial site of a Pre-Quiche Indian tribe was credited to him, and he was at once appointed Official Investigator of Pre-Columbian Civilizations by the perplexed mayor of the town.

Beaming with pride at the site of the old jail, Don Fidelio promised in his acceptance speech to dedicate his life to digging.

IX

ON THE ROAD TO QUIRIGUA

I am convinced that the roads have moods of their own.

There are roads shared by trees and laced with wild flowers, and roads scarred by sadness that carry dead animals on their shoulders–some dead longer than others. There are roads that like to be traveled, and roads that aren't kind to men.

Freddy was the driver of the Volkswagen camper that coughed its way through the dryness of the easterly wastelands of Guatemala, where nothing grows but deformed cacti, which seemed lost in the desert.

It was noon. The sky, tinted a sickly blue, extended itself forever, dying of aloneness.

Freddy was as alone as the sky. His pale blue eyes posed on the land with indifference. He had thin lips that never smiled and a tattoo of blond white beard, which never grew. He was agile but moved slowly; his body, no longer young, had the strength of rusting wire. He had been German at one time. Now he had forgotten what it meant to be of any country.

He was my driver for hire. We were driving to Quirigua, the land where the Maya built tall monoliths with engravings of strange animal gods that ruled the afterlife before Christ. Nine stelae were carved with dots and lines–like telegrams in Morse–and personages holding in their cupped hands small figures of men.

"Are you hungry or shall we wait?"

Freddy spoke Spanish without an accent.

"What are we going to eat?"

"We may stop somewhere; it's not far to Estanzuela."

"Not close to anywhere. What are we going to eat?"

"Coffee," he said. "*Café*."

"*Café*," I echoed.

We drove in silence chewing thoughts that tasted bitter.

Without notice he stopped the car and then backed up a short distance. He opened the glove compartment and brought out a newspaper bundle tied carefully with a string.

"Flowers," he explained. "Flowers for the dead." He unwrapped the package and fluffed several red plastic roses and green foliage arranged in a bouquet. He pointed to a small cross near a rock on the road shoulder. "I always bring her flowers; when you are a driver on this road, it's good to keep the dead content."

Someone had died on the road; the cross marked the site but gave no name or date. It only marked the place. Now the cross, the austerity despoiled by the plastic flowers, looked grotesque, as if dressed up for a *fiesta*.

"Soon we will reach Estanzuela," he repeated. "We can eat there. They have a museum with the bones of a mastodon which they found nearby–I mean they found the skeleton, not the live animal." He was meticulous in his descriptions.

"'Achtung'!" I said, mockingly. "You must always be precise!" I spoke softly, but saw my words whipped his face.

"It's my nature," he said reflectively. "It was a mistake." He looked at me sadly. "You haven't forgiven."

I knew what he was talking about. He had grown among us. A child bronzed by our sun, he swam in our rivers; he had eaten our food and spoken our language. He had run with us to the railroad station to guess and bet on how soon a train would arrive by pressing our ears to the rails, and in the evenings, at the plaza across from the church, he had played Cera–a game with small round black bee-wax cakes–and marbles. He and I had been friends!

Then one day he was no longer one of us, nor was he my friend. He had become a "Hitlerjunge," an Aryan child, dressed in short brown trousers, aloof and cruelly distant, indifferent to our love, our rivers and our land. "We can't be friends," he told me as we met secretly behind the church. "I belong to the Aryan and you are"–he groped for a word–"you are a Jew." Only a child can break another child's heart.

He left our country but returned defeated. The land took him back and nursed him again to health. Fifty years had passed.

"Fifty years, and you have not forgiven."

"Yes, fifty years and still I am a Jew."

The empty land kept mocking the horizon; distance is made of hopes or despair.

Estanzuela was almost lost amid pastures dried by the sun. A pale town, her face whitewashed clean, she stood on her toes a few feet above the sea. Her empty streets smelled of baked dust and at times of burning diesel fuel, coughed in spasms by decrepit buses escaping away from Estanzuela.

The town's sky was mottled by small vultures searching for carrion. The time of greatness had passed Estanzuela eons before, when mastodons roamed lands.

"Are you hungry, or shall we wait?"

"What are we going to eat?"

The Volkswagen camper drove slowly through the streets, like a dog scenting lampposts.

"It says there, *'Café'*."

"Shall we stop?"

A woman dressed in black moved between four tables set in a patio of brown bricks. She had washed them that morning and now steam floated from them.

"*Café*?" she asked.

"*Si*," one of us answered.

The woman left. She was not old, but her shadow was bent.

"One changes much in fifty years."

I felt his eyes searching my gestures.

"Who accuses you?" I asked.

"I have no accusers. They are dead."

"Then you will have to speak for them." I looked at him with compassion.

"It's not easy," said Freddy. "I can't hear their voices; I can't remember their faces."

"What can you hear?"

"Only their cries. They didn't believe what was happening.... They couldn't believe."

"Nobody in the world could believe it either."

"I still hear them at night, their muffled cries."

"Why do you tell me?" He was burdening me with his anguish.

"I thought perhaps you could talk to them. Tell them of my repentance."

"Why don't you tell them yourself?"

"They will not listen to me. They cease crying and their silence is worse than their cries."

The woman brought steaming coffee in a clay pot.

"Will you be eating now?"

"We will wait," Freddy said.

The afternoon weighed heavily on Estanzuela. The patio with the four square tables remained clean, sad and empty.

Freddy stood up, as if he had heard someone call his name.

"It's not in my nature to wait without a purpose. I must fill up the camper with gasoline."

"Will you be long?" I asked, just for asking.

"I will stop at the museum, to see the mastodon."

"Bring him flowers," I said, and regretted my words.

"I won't be long."

I looked at his face as he stood there adjusting his small cap with visor; his expression reminded me of Van Gogh's self-portrait after his mutilation. He walked away, unbending and rhythmic, like a toy soldier.

Yes, I reflected, it's in his nature.

I tried to read, but my thoughts rebelled, so I closed my book. The story of the Cahuac Sky, the last king of Copan, would have to wait. My eyes closed and I drifted into a sweet penumbra.

Suddenly, a sharp sound, like the crack of a whip, threw a handful of frightened birds against the sky.

The woman in black appeared and came toward me.

"Did you hear the shot?" She crossed herself.

"Perhaps a car backfired."

She listened with head cocked like a crow; there were no other sounds. She smiled, tranquilized.

"I didn't think of that. I have not been myself. Will you eat now or wait for your companion to return?"

"I will wait."

From her skirt pocket she brought out the stub of a candle that she lit and turned on its side until the melted wax fell on the table, then stuck the candle to it.

"To scare the flies," she explained. "It keeps them away. Don't ask me why."

She looked at me, smiling. Her handsome brown face was marred by neglect.

"Why do you dress in black?" I asked.

"I am a widow. My man was killed on the road to Quirigua–hit and run they called it.... He died by the road as a dog."

"How long will you mourn?"

"All my life. I would be mortified if my husband came to visit me, and I wasn't wearing black."

"But you said you are a widow. Do you have a new husband?"

"No, it's the same husband. It's only that he now lives in the other world."

She said *en el otro mundo*, and in Spanish, the world of the dead seemed closer, part of the neighborhood.

"Is there *un otro mundo*?"

"I only know what my husband tells me *cuando me visita*."

"When he visits you...?"

"He visits me *en sueños y murmullos*." She smiled caressing the words.

"In dreams and whispers. In the darkness of night?"

"There's no darkness or light for the dead, no love nor hate, that's why their home is called eternity."

Moving closer to me, she whispered confidentially. "They come to visit because they want to teach. They like to teach." She raised her upturned hands in a gesture of resignation. "*Pobrecitos*. They don't know we cannot learn."

A knock at the door interrupted us. She went to answer it, returning with a man in a uniform, to whom she pointed me out.

"He is the companion."

"Your companion...*Señor*," the officer began. He took his cap off and brought it to his chest.

X

LUCIA BETWEEN THE SHADOWS

Don Julio was very disconcerted. His handsome face, with sad black Indian eyes and droopy mustache, revealed fear, curiosity and awe.

"Luciiiaaa!" His voice trailed into a yodel as he moved from one end to the other in the garden of his restaurant, lighting luminaries on top of blue tables and straightening chairs with raffia seats. The tables were scattered among lemon and orange trees, and under taller trees embraced by climbing vines with leaves large as Chinese parasols.

He moved with great agility for a portly man.

"Where could that child be?" he asked. "She appears and disappears in less time than it takes to bat an eye."

"Maybe she is turning out to be like her grandfather," Uno answered. Lucia's old grandfather had been a well-known shaman. It was claimed he also was a *characotel*, a warlock who could become a deer, a snake or a coyote at will, to escape enemies or to carry out his vengeances.

"*Que Dios no lo permita*. All I need is to have a child witch under my roof!" protested Don Julio, and he crossed himself hurriedly. "This is turning from light chestnut to dark. Four times she has disappeared right in front of my eyes, into thin air, so to speak, and twice more in front of my wife's eyes." He counted with his fingers convincingly. "This makes six times."

"Why are you howling like a coyote?" Lucia's child-sweet voice came from a corner of the garden. She carried an armful of mint, marjoram and thyme. "I was picking my herbs." She dropped the herbs on a table and scratched her head.

"Where?" Don Julio asked in exasperation. "I swear I looked for you everywhere!"

"In the corner by the guava tree. I saw you walk right by me." Her irreverent white teeth scattered with a smile. "I was hiding behind the cat." She picked up the herbs and went into the kitchen, still scratching, leaving the perplexed Don Julio standing before Uno and me, with hands dangling helplessly from his powerful body like mangoes from a tree.

Lucia spoke in halting Spanish. Her native tongue was *Quiche*. She was a small girl for her age, which was only twelve, dressed in the colors of her tribe: blue, orange and red. Her black hair was braided with green ribbons and she had large, frightened black eyes and very white teeth, which had grown in total disarray.

Her village had been burned a year before by soldiers, who suspected the villages of harboring guerrilla men. A brutal war raped the land, leaving a trail of orphans. Lucia had been found hiding in the branches of a tree by a sergeant who took the child to Don Julio's household and left her there, like a parcel from a post office. Lucia remained and became a servant-child at Don Julio's home in Panimache.

Panimache, the hidden village in the Guatemalan highlands, drank her beauty in the waters of Lake Atitlan, and by a miracle of miracles was never disturbed by the war.

Lucia's acceptance had not been easy for Don Julio and his wife, Rosarita. In the villager's eyes Indian children were pagan, and invariably invaded by *piojitos* and *diablitos*–little lice and tiny devils. Don Bruno, the village priest, helped with the *diablitos*. He promptly baptized her, and so neither Lucia nor Don Julio nor Doña Rosarita was ever bothered by tiny devils.

The *piojitos* were a different story. Lucia bathed daily and braided her hair meticulously after pulling it through a closely meshed comb and yet, even though the little lice disappeared, the *piojitos* in her mind never abandoned her. As pretty a child as she was, Lucia seemed always to be scratching away her invisible *piojitos*.

Don Julio was a good Catholic, which in village parlance meant that his wife went to church on Sundays. His own participation was limited to Holy Week when, with other members of his confraternity, he helped carry a movable altar of "Jesus Crucified" through the tortuous streets of the village. Yet, in spite of this public proclamation of faith, Don Julio kept in a corner of his garden a small Indian idol, and occasionally when the breeze from the lake was weak one could smell the sweet aroma of burning incense.

Don Julio was a man of many contradictions. Don Bruno, the village priest, understood the duality of his friend's faith, accepting half of his conversion rather than none–a very different attitude from that of Miss Fanny Rameriz Davis, director of the only school in the village, who kept a gelid distance from anything faintly suggestive of impropriety. The grandchild of an English adventurer who planted his seed in Indian soil, Doña Fanita, as she was popularly called, kept a reverent memory of her buccaneer grandfather with the fanatical devotion of a museum curator. Doña Fanita was tall and had inherited the bad teeth and equine face of her ancestor, but, in all fairness, she was an excellent teacher. The Davis in her name promptly opened for her the doors of village society, and soon the parents of her many disciples followed her advice without question. In matters of education and social acceptance, Miss Fanny R. Davis became the supreme arbiter.

It is the law, eternal and immutable, that when opposite forces occupy the same space, catastrophe follows.

From the beginning it was an unfair contest. The child Lucia was refused acceptance to the school because she was not baptized, but even after Don Bruno corrected the deficiency, Doña Fanny found many reasons to keep the little Indian from her school and so ran into a confrontation with Don Julio.

"You realize," he said, "I had no candle to hold in this wake. These things are always better handled by women. But it's not my way to see children trampled and just stand by, counting the stars in heaven or figuring the number of notes in a cock's crow."

He organized a *huelga*, a boycott of sorts. Every morning he rode his bicycle to the school entrance and passed out by hand yellow leaflets on which, printed in black characters, were the words: *Abajo con el Malinchismo*.

Now, not many knew that *Abajo* means "Down with," and even fewer understood *Malinchismo*, a word imported from Mexico that refers to the subservience of natives to foreigners. Malinche was the name of the Aztec maiden given to Cortez as a gift from Moctezuma. She converted to Christianity and became a Spanish ally against her own people. Thus her name became descriptive of the attitude of servility to foreigners.

As strikes go, Don Julio's was doomed from the start. No one in the village wished to be a native. Claims to foreign nobility flew to life like so many moths. Don Julio's restaurant, El Gallo Contento, which took pride in its native cuisine, became deserted, while Il Bistro Parmesiano owned by Signora Donna Palmieri, Le Chateau de la Normandie, The Giant Squid, and Trafalgar Square were suddenly invaded by many beautiful brown Mayan faces affecting tastes foreign to their tongues.

Uno and I were among the last surviving customers at Don Julio's restaurant, and now, under the enticing light of a coquettish moon, we listened to his strange story.

"No," Don Julio repeated, "I held no candle in this wake." He looked first to Uno and then to me. "I'm not a partisan to causes. Too many tragedies start out as good causes. But every day, when I saw Lucia's eyes trail the children on their way to school, carrying their books and wearing their pretty uniforms, something broke up inside of me. She would then feed the chickens and count aloud the grains of maize. She could count to sixteen because my wife Rosarita taught her. After that she threw handfuls, repeating 'sixteen, sixteen...' And when she did that, I felt that every little grain was like a bullet hurting my chest."

Don Julio shook his head slowly, like an ox. "*Con mil perdones*," he said. "Forgive me a thousand times for invading your table. I have even forgotten my manners."

"Please, Don Julio," Uno said, "sit down with us, if you have a moment to spare."

"*Con mucho gusto*, Señor Uno y Señor Quince. *Permitan me que les invite un traguito.*" He went into the kitchen and returned promptly with a bottle of Anis del Mono and three small glasses, and poured the anisette carefully.

"Every morning as the children went by," he continued, "Lucia counted aloud her maize grains, proud of what she had learned, until one day when the children destroyed her dream. As she counted, they chanted with her, '*Uno, dos, tres, cuatro...diez y seis...*' mocking her ignorance and Indian intonation. Lucia tried to hide in the doorway, making herself small, like a wounded sparrow."

Don Julio took a sip of his anisette and slapped his face. "*Chingados mosquitoes!*" He cursed invisible gnats. "That's when all this disappearing started. Maybe she escaped back to the only school she knew–her grandfather's school–and like him she started hiding."

"I knew him," Uno interrupted softly. "He was a *characotel*. He could hide in the form of any animal he wished, better than anyone else."

"But, do wizards become animals themselves?" I asked.

"No," Uno said. "They hide behind the form of the animals. Sometimes it's a snake, a black bird or a coyote. They remain themselves, because human nature cannot lower itself to that of an animal, but they hide behind their forms. It's impossible to understand how this mystery works."

"In the beginning, I didn't want to believe my eyes," Don Julio continued, "but one needs to be blind not to see what is happening. Lucia already knows how to hide like a bird or a cat, and she is still learning. She appears and disappears at will." Don Julio smiled, a gold tooth shining in the moonlight. "My wife tells me that when the chores in the kitchen become boring, Lucia suddenly vanishes, and a blue jay flies off the windowsill."

Don Julio poured us another small glass of anisette. "Do you enjoy your *traguito*?" he asked, very pleased by his treat.

"My very favorite," Uno said. He took the bottle and examined the label. "Anis del Mono," he read. "Have you noticed that the ape in the label looks more like an old man than he does an ape?"

We all took turns examining the bottle. Uno was right. The grotesque image looked like a hairy old man with a tail.

The silence of the night was faintly broken by the distant howl of a coyote. As if in answer, a light noise in the brush caught our attention. It was a cat, a yellow cat, walking with deliberate care. She reached our table and stood for a moment, then continued her excursion into the night.

Uno smiled and looked at me. Don Julio crossed himself.

For several weeks it seemed El Gallo Contento would go out of business. The only customers could be counted on the fingers of one hand. There was Don Bruno and Mike, the American who owned The Giant Squid, but liked Don Julio's food better than his own. Uno and I completed the quartet.

Little Lucia knew the reason for the scarcity of customers. She was only a child. The battle among grownups confused her. Once more she felt abandoned and guilty, as she had when her village was burned. She felt it was her sin, the original sin Don Bruno had spoken of, and so, her anguished eyes asking forgiveness, she worked to meet the smallest wishes of the few patrons, moving anxiously from table to table, guessing needs.

At night, alone in her room, she hid in fear. She hid behind the shapes of birds and behind the small forms of little predators who hunted in the dark.

Meanwhile, like an embattled Don Quijote riding a Raleigh bicycle instead of Rocinante, Don Julio continued his pamphleteering crusade, distributing every morning his yellow leaflets with the proclamation: *Abajo con el Malinchismo*. A few neighbors grew curious about the strange word and asked for an explanation, but the immense majority continued to boycott his business and to side with Doña Fanita.

Gradually, as business went from bad to worse, the offerings of incense to the idol in the garden increased, and, perhaps because of that, or because the prayers of Don Bruno found an answer, or because, after all, human beings are ruled by the law of the stomach, a change took place.

Furtively, the servants of Doña Fanita's supporters appeared at the restaurant in the evenings asking for take-out orders of Don Julio's specialties. The scaloppini of veal Baronick from Signora Palmieri was a sad competitor for Don Julio's *paches Quetzaltecos*, and his chiles rellenos ran circles around the *fruits de mer Chez Sal* specialty of Le Chateau de la Normandie. The hamburgers from The Giant Squid fared a little better, but had to concede to *carne asada con salsa de chipotle*. Trafalgar Square, with its fish and chips, was never a serious contender.

In a coup of inspired strategy, Don Julio adamantly refused to accept take-out orders, and so the proud villagers came back slowly, one by one, to the Gallo Contento to once more enjoy the delicacies they had missed, and to sit among the lemon trees. As Doña Fanita found her supporters faltering, in a bout of inherited English wisdom she wrote a letter stating how happy the school would be to accept Lucia as a new student.

Once more the village breathed peace and contentment.

But Lucia couldn't be found.

She was not in the kitchen, nor in the garden. Don Julio then took to the streets on his bicycle, waving his letter like a tiny peace flag, but Lucia was not there. And she was not by the lake...nor on the hill where coyotes gather at night...nor by the river where she learned to count by throwing pebbles into the water. Nor was she at the cascade, where the water poured into the abyss. The abyss!

"Luciiiaaa!" Don Julio's voice was lost in the terrible roar of falling water.

But there was no answer.

Lucia had learned to hide behind her own shadow, and no one ever saw her again.

Works Cited

Daffodils, William Wordsworth, http://www.poetry-online.org/wordsworth_daffodils.htm

Die Leiden Des Jungen Werther, Johann Wolfgang von Goethe, http://www.gutenberg.org/wiki/Gutenberg:Terms_of_Use

Ecclesiasticus, The Bible, Douay-Rheims, Book 26, http://www.gutenberg.org/ebooks/8326

Hosea, The World English Bible, http://www.gutenberg.org/dirs/etext05/web2810h.htm

La Familia de Pascual Duarte, Camilo Jose Cela, http://en.wikipedia.org/wiki/The_Family_of_Pascual_Duarte

La Suave Patria, Ramon Lopez Velarde, http://www.poemasde.net/la-suave-patria-ramon-lopez-velarde/

Pagliacci, Ruggero Leoncavallo, http://en.wikipedia.org/wiki/Pagliacci

Rain, Maugham, W. Somerset, http://maugham.classicauthors.net/Rain/

Song of Solomon, The Bible, http://www.gutenberg.org/dirs/etext05/web2210h.htm

Thaïs, Anatole France, http://www.gutenberg.org/wiki/Gutenberg:Terms_of_Use

The Death of the Hired Man, Robert Frost, http://www.bartleby.com/118/3.html

The Stolen Child, William Butler Yeats, (n.d.), http://www.brainyquote.com/quotes/quotes/w/williambut

www.ingramcontent.com/pod-product-compliance
Lightning Source LLC
Chambersburg PA
CBHW050929120626
46552CB00001B/120